## praise for *spacetime donuts*

"Hip, humorous, and refreshing."
—*American Book Review*

"It's all done up in great style and it marks an auspicious debut."—*Roanoke Times & World-News*

"[Rucker] knows how to boggle the mind and, next chapter, to boggle it again."—Thomas M. Disch, author of *Camp Concentration* and *334*

"*Spacetime Donuts* possesses an off-the-wall comedic genius that one rarely stumbles across, yet can fall immediately in love with . . . I wish more fiction were this fun."—*Speculiction*

# praise for rudy rucker

"Rudy Rucker should be declared a National Treasure of American Science Fiction. Someone simultaneously channeling Kurt Gödel and Lenny Bruce might start to approximate full-on Ruckerian warp-space, but without the sweet, human, splendidly goofy Rudyness at the core of the singularity." —William Gibson

"One of science fiction's wittiest writers. A genius . . . a cult hero among discriminating cyberpunkers." —*San Diego Union-Tribune*

"Rucker's writing is great like the Ramones are great: a genre stripped to its essence, attitude up the wazoo, and cartoon sentiments that reek of identifiable lives and issues. Wild math you can get elsewhere, but no one does the cyber version of beatnik glory quite like Rucker." —*New York Review of Science Fiction*

"What a Dickensian genius Rucker has for Californian characters, as if, say, Dickens had fused with Phil Dick and taken up surfing and jamming and topologising. He has a hotline to cosmic revelations yet he's always here and now in the groove, tossing off lines of beauty and comic wisdom. 'My heart is a dog running after every cat.' We really feel with his characters in their bizarre tragicomic quests." —Ian Watson, author of *The Embedding*

"The current crop of sf humorists are mildly risible, I suppose, but they don't seem to pack the same intellectual punch of their forebears. With one exception, that is: the astonishing Rudy Rucker. For some two decades now, since the publication of his first novel, *White Light*, Rucker has combined an easygoing, trippy style influenced by the Beats with a deep engagement with knotty (or 'gnarly,' to employ one of his favorite terms) intellectual conceits, based mainly in mathematics. In the typical Rucker novel, likably eccentric characters—who run the gamut from brilliant to near-certifiable—encounter aspects of the universe that confirm that life is weirder than we can imagine." —*The Washington Post*

"Rucker stands alone in the science fiction pantheon as some kind of trickster god of the computer science lab; where others construct minutely plausible fictional realities, he simply grabs the corners of the one we already know and twists it in directions we don't have pronounceable names for." —*SF Site*

"Reading a Rudy Rucker book is like finding Poe, Kerouac, Lewis Carroll, and Philip K. Dick parked on your driveway in a topless '57 Caddy . . . and telling you they're taking you for a RIDE. The funniest science fiction author around." —*Sci-Fi Universe*

"This is SF rigorously following crazy rules. My mind of science fiction. At the heart of it is a rage to extrapolate. Rucker is what happens when you cross a mathematician with the extrapolating jazz spirit." —Robert Sheckley

"Rucker [gives you] more ideas per chapter than most authors use in an entire novel." —*San Francisco Chronicle*

"Rudy Rucker writes like the love child of Philip K. Dick and George Carlin. Brilliant, frantic, conceptual, cosmological . . . like lucid dreaming, only funny." —*New York Times* bestselling author Walter Jon Williams

# by rudy rucker

## FICTION

## NON-FICTION

# spacetime donuts

### a novel by

# RUDY RUCKER

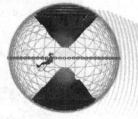

**night shade books**
**new york**

First edition: Paperback, Ace Books 1981
Second edition: Paperback and ebook, E-Reads, 2008
Third edition: Paperback and ebook, Transreal Books, 2016
First Night Shade Books edition published 2019

Visit our website at www.nightshadebooks.com.

10 9 8 7 6 5 4 3 2 1

Library of Congress Cataloging-in-Publication Data

Names: Rucker, Rudy v. B. (Rudy von Bitter), 1946- author.
Title: Spacetime donuts / Rudy Rucker.
Description: First Night Shade Books edition. | New York : Night Shade Books, 2019.
Identifiers: LCCN 2018041196 | ISBN 9781597809979 (pbk. : alk. paper)
Subjects: | GSAFD: Science fiction.
Classification: LCC PS3568.U298 S74 2019 | DDC 813/.54--dc23
LC record available at https://lccn.loc.gov/2018041196

Cover artwork by Bill Carman
Cover design by Claudia Noble

Printed in the United States of America

For Kurt Gödel, Mick Jagger and 1972

# contents

# welcome to the gnarl zone
## an introduction by richard kadrey

I first met Rudy Rucker in Los Gatos, California, shortly after he and his family moved there from Virginia. We met because *Interzone* magazine wanted me to interview him. He was still in Lynchburg when I wrote and asked if he was willing to talk about his work. At the time, Rudy was in the last throes of house-packing panic, so his note back to me was scrawled on a ripped scrap of paper and looked like something a hostage might smuggle out of an underground bunker to let his rescuers know that he was still alive. I wish I still had that gnarled little thing. It would be a nice keepsake and it was a perfect introduction to Rudy's world of gnarl. But more on that later.

Before moving into computer science, Rudy spent many years as a math teacher. Sure, it says so in his bio, but I lived it firsthand. When we met, I'd just heard about these things called "fractals." I knew they were important and I knew that I should get to know them better, but I also knew that fractals involved numbers, and my fear of math was even greater than that of spiders and cops. But Rudy changed all that. (The math part. He couldn't make me like spiders or cops.) On a short walk up a steep hill by his house, he broke down fractals in a way that even my trembling brain meat could understand. Later, he showed me some Cellular Automata and fractal-generating programs he'd written. Suddenly, math was no longer a source of infinite frustration, but something full of beauty and mystery. That was Rudy the teacher. The thing is, though, Rudy the teacher isn't all that removed from Rudy the writer.

Along with authors like Bruce Sterling, William Gibson, Jon Shirley, Lewis Shiner, and Pat Cadigan, Rudy was one of the original cyberpunks. (If you don't know what cyberpunk is, read Rudy's *Software* and *Wetware* for a crash course.) Like those other writers, Rudy had an innate ability to combine human characters with edgy science and social commentary in new ways. In the rush of those early cyberpunk works, Rudy's stood apart because of the humor and surprising plot structures. I once heard him talk about drawing mazes for his kids, how you could start out thinking you knew the proper way to construct the thing, but twists and turns would always surprise you. Then, you had to back up and erase some stuff before moving forward again. That's how Rudy's books were written, part planning and part improvisation when he hit a wall or unexpected turn. It's what he refers to as *gnarl*.

What is gnarl? First off, it's a surfing term. Waves have gnarl and a gnarly wave is a good one you can ride all the way back to shore. Most of the time. Gnarl can surprise you. The way he describes gnarl it's "a level of complexity that lies between predictability and randomness." Also,

"The gnarl zone lies at the interface of logic and fantasy." Those are probably the best descriptions of Rudy's fiction you'll find anywhere. But there's more.

Rudy wasn't just a cyberpunk. He'd also developed his own alternate writing method, something he dubbed Transrealism. He describes Transrealism as not a new style of SF, but "a type of avant-garde literature." The realism comes from infusing the story with both the personality of the writer, but also people the writer knows, primarily friends and family members. This anchors any heavy weirdness in the real world. The "trans" part of Transrealism comes from using wild science or even magic to twist whatever points of reality the writer wants to look at, while simultaneously commenting on them. At least, that was early Transrealism. Even Rudy's own invention couldn't hold him forever. Over time, Transrealism morphed into a new, more mature form in which the author no longer needed to insert him or herself, but simply to bring in emotions and perceptions that they've personally experienced. The "trans" part now occurs when the writer "raises the action to a higher level ... choosing tropes so as to intensify and augment some artistically chosen aspects of reality." After all his years as a writer, Rudy remains a teacher, only now he's teaching himself new forms and approaches to work. I have no doubt that in a few years, Transrealism will go through another transformation and emerge as an even more personal and weirder form.

All of which leads us to the book you're holding in your hands, *Spacetime Donuts*. It's the transreal tale of

Vernor Maxwell in an oppressive zero-needs society and his attempt to break out of the clutches of Phizwhiz, the all-knowing, all-seeing supercomputer that runs his world. To plan his escape, Vernor brings together his friends, the mysterious professor Kurtowski, plus a lot of math, sex, and drugs. Vernor believes that reality is circular and that if you go small enough, like really, really, really small, you will expand to the size of the universe, but eventually return to your original size and back in the real world. Imagine a smarter, funnier version of *The Incredible Shrinking Man* mixed with what I think is a kind of *Alice in Wonderland* approach to reality, and laced with the science to make it all come together. *Spacetime Donuts* is also a very personal book because it's covertly about Rudy's time as a grad student, an encounter with Kurt Gödel, and a mind-altering acid trip.

That's really all you need to know about the book because Rudy *is* the book and the book *is* Rudy. He's a kind and generous man who once sat in a tree, after smoking copious amounts of weed, thinking about math and mysticism—and was almost sucked up into infinity's endless, timeless maw. But he stayed with us mortals and we got the novel you're holding right now. If that isn't enough to make you want to read the thing, I don't know what the hell is wrong with you. But if you want to stay up late and, like the best rock and roll, run around and break things—reality, for instance—you should try a Spacetime Donut. You'll be gobbling time, space, and the universe itself. Grab hold, take a bite, and enjoy the ride.

# spacetime donuts

part one

part one

# prologue

They called it "Us" then instead of "America." As in the popular slogan, "Us is Users and Users is Us." The Governor said that in most of his speeches; which always ended, "Us needs you 'cause you're Younique."

Which was a load of crap, natch. There were Drones and there were Dreamers, and that was about as unique as it got.

The Drones lived in robot-built suburbs. In the daytime they rode the walk-tubes to their offices in the City. Their main job was to fill out probing questionnaires.

The Dreamers lived together in vast apartment blocks. It was easy to spot a Dreamer because of the socket in the base of the skull. If you were a Dreamer, you plugged a wire like a phone cord into that socket every night.

The Drones' questionnaires and the Dreamers' brain-waves all ended up inside Phizwhiz, a vast network of linked computers and robots. Phizwhiz always knew what the Users wanted. If what they wanted was impossible or unsafe, then it was Phizwhiz's job to change the Users' minds before they found out that they wanted something impossible or unsafe. Phizwhiz did this by continually adjusting the Hollows, which everyone watched.

Hollows were holograms ... three-dimensional, full-color, life-size images which talked and flickered all day long. Everyone had a small padded room called the "Nest" with a Hollows receiver on the floor. In your Nest you could lean against the soft wall and be on a yacht in the Mediterranean, or alone with the Governor while he told you a secret; at the scene of a Public Safety raid, or in bed with a friendly and beautiful couple.

It was all so real that the Users—Drones and Dreamers alike—wanted little else from life. Which was just as well, since Phizwhiz had come to do all the real work there was to do. This was partly because of human laziness, and partly because Phizwhiz had been programmed to value human life above all else. People had tended to hurt themselves when they worked in factories, fields, and laboratories. So by the time 2165 rolled around, Phizwhiz had it set up so that the average User never touched the controls of anything more dangerous than a cold-water tap.

It was an easy life, and with Phizwhiz picking your brain and manipulating the Hollows, you'd usually been psyched into dropping a gripe before you knew you had it. Usually. But there were some problems which were hard to forget about. Like the fact that the machines never did anything quite right. And the fact that there were no real changes anymore. No new inventions, no new ideas, not even any really new shows on the Hollows. Phizwhiz was happy, but Us was bored.

It occurred to someone that Phizwhiz might be more creative if a few human brains could be built into the network. The Governor appealed to the Dreamers to come plug their brains into Phizwhiz's full logical space, and a few ambitious volunteers turned up.

This kind of hook-up was something quite different from the gingerly probing of the Dream Machine, that electronic poll-taker which nightly monitored the collective response of the Dreamers' brains to various weak currents and waveforms. In fact, the incredible thought amplification and information overload experienced upon *full* brain interlock with Phizwhiz turned all of the sane and healthy people who tried it into drooling undesirables instants after they plugged in.

It began to look like the Users were stuck with their tepid, steady-state society. But then the Angels appeared.

# ONE
# vernor maxwell

Vernor Maxwell grew up in a Dreamtown high-rise. When he was thirteen his father took him in to get his plug installed, and the family was awarded a new receiver for the Hollownest. At first the plug frightened him, and he would lie awake for hours while the alien images and sensations trickled into his brain from the Dream Machine. Soon, however, he began to feel a certain pleasure, almost sexual, at the dark nightly joining of his mind with all the others. Sometimes he would imagine bright impulses passing out of his plug, through the Dream Machine, and into some young girl's pure brain. The older kids bragged about actually plugging their brains directly into their girlfriends' brains, and they would show Vernor the short lengths of coaxial cable which they used.

There was no school; the Hollows' morning line-up of kiddie shows provided all the education that the Users' children would ever need. No one checked if the kids watched the shows, but they didn't have to. The shows were fun, and Vernor rarely missed them. When he got bored he would

fool with the controls on the Hollow receiver until the
Nest was filled with flying blobs of light and fragmented
images. After awhile his mother would come in and yell at
him to fix it. He would retune so that the Hollows took on
their normal wavering and grainy appearance, then go out
in the street to play with his friends.

By the time he was sixteen, the "play" consisted mainly
of getting twisted on tranks and seeweed. Users generally took the two together, trans-steroid tranquilizers
and reefers of seeweed. Seeweed was a mutated aquatic
strain of *cannabis sativa*. All you had to do was drop a seed
into a bucket of urine, and six weeks later you had a half-
pound of seeweed. The grownups said you'd go crazy if
you smoked it without taking tranks to smooth the trip,
and they may have been right; but the kids continued to
function pretty well after they discovered that tranks just
took the edge off the weed.

A lot of Dreamer kids were into electricity, too, feeding it raw in through their skull plugs. You could hook a
regular dry-cell battery to your plug; it would make you
come for half an hour if you did it right . . . and pass out in
convulsions if you did it wrong. Of course, batteries were
illegal, but they weren't too hard to get. Not much harder
than the drugs, which *were* legal for anyone over eighteen.
Legal and illegal were not, after all, very important concepts in Dreamtown. The City had a police force, known
collectively as the loach, but the loach tended to stay out
of Dreamtown. The Hollows kept down any large-scale
unrest which the Dream Machine detected, and most
Dreamers didn't own anything worth stealing.

The more sophisticated kids sent *pulsed* electricity from hand-cranked dynamos in through their plugs and called themselves electrofreaks. Vernor tried it a couple of times, had an epileptic fit, and gave it up. He had begun to wish he didn't have a plug at all. There was a passive, addicted feeling to plugging in every night, and lying there hooked in with all the other Dreamers, fleshly components of Phizwhiz. After spending a night with the soft knob at the back of your neck, while thoughts and feelings ebbed and flowed through the coiled cable, you never really knew what they had put in and what they had taken out. Some mornings you felt like you had dreamed everyone's dream, all tangled together, and you couldn't meet peoples' eyes . . . but no one talked about it.

When he was twenty, Vernor started hanging around the library. Since there were so many people and so few real jobs, there was no encouragement to be anything other than a Dreamer, but if you were interested, you could study just about anything with the recorded Hollowcasts in the library. Vernor was interested in science, and he went through most of the introductory science courses which had been saved on infocubes. Physics and mathematics attracted him in particular, and soon he had exhausted the library's supply of infocubes in these areas.

It became necessary to learn how to read. The Hollow shows had taught him letters, numbers, and the phonetic reading of short words, but he had never actually read a book. The first book he read was Abbott's *Flatland*, and its archaic language and bizarre ideas fired his imagination. Months ran into years as he pursued his studies of

Quantum Mechanics, General Field Theory, Geometro-dynamics, Relativistic Cosmology, Mathematical Logic, and the Philosophy of Science. And sometimes, for a break, he'd study the history of Dadaism and Surrealism—he was a particular fan of Marcel Duchamp.

He discovered that if he slept on a table, the cleaning robots would not disturb him, so he began spending his nights in the library. That way he no longer had to plug into the Dream Machine. If he slept at home it was impossible not to plug in, for the bed had a weight sensor which set off a "reminder bell" if the bed's occupant wasn't properly jacked in.

There was even a Dreamfood tap in the library's lounge, so he soon stopped going home entirely. When he told his parents he was living in the library, they were proud . . . until they discovered that Vernor was not learning a technical skill which might give him a chance of someday having a job. Being a Dreamer was, of course, a job of sorts . . . every day's Hollowcast to Dreamtown ended with a slogan intended to encourage this belief: "Us needs you 'cause you're Younique!" But no amount of propaganda, no number of Hollows of the President saying, "Us is Users. Dream Us our tomorrow." could erase the Dreamers' sad and hidden knowledge of their uselessness.

But to study physics and mathematics? What was the good of that? There were no physicists any more, although being a physicist was not expressly illegal. What *was* illegal was to conduct experiments in a laboratory. It was too dangerous . . . dangerous to the experimenter, and dangerous to the society that he might use his new discoveries on. Mathematics and theoretical physics were legal, but no one would pay people to do them; the common conception being that Phizwhiz was much better at science than any human could be.

Like all common conceptions about science, this was false. Phizwhiz was not much of a scientist. He knew enough to question old hypotheses, but he had no access to that inner vision of the Absolute which shines through the work of the true scientist.

Vernor had heard of the Us's attempts to give Phizwhiz soul by plugging him into certain Dreamers' minds, and he sometimes felt that if anyone would ever be able to survive such an experience it would be Vernor Maxwell. He took many strange trips lying on his library table, smoking seeweed or tripping on LSD. He had seen the world go solid and shatter into dust, leaving only a pure shimmer of abstract relations. He had watched the gnat of his consciousness speed urgently across his inner landscape as another part of himself tried to catch and dissect it, naming all the parts for once and all. He no longer could tell the difference between a good trip and a bad trip . . . or rather this artificial distinction had fallen away.

One day the news spread that a man had entered into full communication with Phizwhiz and survived. Vernor watched him in the Hollownest of a bar near the library. The man's name was Andy Silver. To the viewer in the Nest, Silver appeared to be leaning against one wall.

Silver had blond hair and a funny way of holding his elbows out from his body. He smiled often, though not necessarily in synchronization with what he was saying

Occasionally he did not appear to know where he was, but this did not seem to disturb him. An invisible voice, which the viewer could imagine to be his own, interviewed Andy Silver.

"Are you the guy that plugged into Phizwhiz last week?"

Silver glanced around, then stared at a spot to Vernor's left. "You bet your ass," he replied.

"What was it like, Andy?"

Silver began pacing around the room, "What's *any*thing like? Real compared to what?" He paused, then continued, "Let's say it's like walking in a garden of light. And every flower is a number. And every number is your name . . ." His voice trailed off and he sat down, looking quietly across the room like a man with all the time in the world.

"How is it, Andy, that you managed to come unscathed through an experience which has shattered the minds of all the others who attempted it?"

"You call this unscathed?" Silver shot back, bursting into laughter, "No, seriously, gate, it was no big deal for me. I've been getting high every day for ten years now so most of my brain's gone anyway . . ." For an instant his eyes rolled and his head seemed to be on fire, but then he continued. "All kidding aside, Jim, I've been studying metamathematics, and actually I was in just the right place to get on top of Phizwhiz. LSD and a good scientific training's all it took. Couldn't have done it without the Professor, though."

"Which Professor are you referring to, Mr. Silver?"

Silver seemed puzzled at the question, but then he gathered himself to recite, "My beloved teacher, Professor G.

Kurtowski, without whose writings and conversations I could never have reached this point."

"Thank you, Andy Silver, the first man to survive a full brain interlock with Phizwhiz. And now, Users, it is our great privilege to welcome the Governor."

The Governor's Hollow walked into the Nest. He was an amazingly evil-looking man who perpetually held his teeth bared in what he imagined to be a smile. Silver gave him the finger, but the Governor brushed past him and stepped forward to buttonhole the Users.

"Always glad to see you," he began, "You're Younique!" His standard opening. He continued, "We are fortunate to have in our fine City a man whose courage and strength of character open before us the exciting vista of a revitalized Phizwhiz."

Silver had turned around so that his back faced the Governor. Curious, Vernor walked across the Hollownest to get on Silver's other side so as to see his face. That was one of the nice things about Hollows, a complete three-dimensional image of the actors was always there in the Nest with you.

Silver was leaning forward confidentially over his cupped right hand. "Hey, man, glad you were hip enough to come over here," he whispered. The Governor was still extolling the bright future in store for the lucky Users in his care. Silver raised his hand and continued, "You know what I got in this hand? zz-74, man. That's what really put me on top. zz-74." He winked, then turned back to his original position facing the Governor's fat, talking back.

zz-74? Vernor had never heard of it before. No one else in the bar's Nest had bothered to go hear Silver's secret message, but surely many others in the City had. zz-74? His attention was drawn back to the Governor's speech.

"We need more Andy Silvers. I urge any citizen who feels able to withstand the titanic mental pressure of merging with the greatest computer the world has ever seen to come forward. Andy Silver is going to put together a team of Dreamers willing and able to get Phizwhiz moving again. More than ever before ... Us is Users and Users is Us!" The Governor seemed about to leave, but struck with a sudden afterthought, he turned to Silver, "Andy, what do you want to call this team?"

Silver looked at the Governor coolly, "The Angels," he said. "We'll be the Angels."

They gave Silver a floor in the main Phizwhiz building downtown, and the next day Vernor was there. Half the Dreamers in town seemed to have gotten there before him. After waiting two hours to get into the building, he gave up and went back to the library. It might, after all, be wise to study some more science and ride out a few more heavy trips before putting his mind on the line. Maybe the whole thing was a hoax, a trick by the Governor to get acid-heads to volunteer for some kind of brain obliteration. Although LSD was legal, it was clear that the Governor disliked freaks.

But Andy Silver's feat was not a hoax, as became evident over the next few months. New gadgets began appearing in the stores. The shows on the Hollows improved greatly. There was a rash of exciting fads. The laws against gardening and painting were dropped, and many people took up these enjoyable, but slightly dangerous hobbies. One man went on a rampage, killing six with his gardening tools, and paintings and slogans which were not good for the public to see began appearing on the sides of buildings and in the walktubes; but Andy Silver prevailed upon Phizwhiz to let the gardening and painting continue. There was even talk of legalizing laboratory science again.

The Us was not entirely happy with all the changes in Phizwhiz's behavior which Andy Silver was bringing about. For his part, Silver made no secret of his revolutionary sentiments . . . occasionally going so far as to state that Phizwhiz should be destroyed. But the public was so enchanted with the life and excitement which he had brought, that it would have been politically impossible to arrest him—even if the Us had been sure it wanted to.

Silver had assembled a core of four other Angels from the many who had volunteered: three men and a woman. Most people never made it past the initial screening, and all the rest, except the four we're talking about, failed the actual machine test . . . losing their minds in the process. Applications for a position with the Angels dropped off drastically as the word of this got around, and Vernor could now have gotten in for a test easily enough, but he hesitated to do this. It would probably be better to get some zz-74 first.

A number of other people had heard Silver mention zz-74 on the Hollows. Lots of people, including the loach, were looking to score some, but there wasn't any around. The general consensus was that zz-74 must be a drug which was being manufactured in an underground laboratory . . . perhaps by the mysterious Professor G. Kurtowski.

Since the Us had not yet been able to obtain and analyze a sample of zz-74, they could not be sure that it was safe, so it was declared illegal, although the government was all too eager to legalize zz-74, if only they could find the formula and swing into production. A good demand for the stuff had built up on the strength of Silver's mention of it, and the Us was not adverse to making hay while the sun shines. They asked, then demanded, that the Angels surrender their cache of the illegal substance, but to no avail. Finally a raid was staged, but no unfamiliar drugs were found in the Angels' possession.

Vernor followed all this with interest, and he began looking into the writings of G. Kurtowski. His early papers were concerned with ironing out various imperfections in the Everett-Wheeler many-universe-interpretation of quantum mechanics. Toward the end of his publishing career, however, a number of surprising empirical predictions had begun to appear in his papers. Vernor was unable to discover if the experiments which Kurtowski suggested had ever been carried out, and Phizwhiz seemed to have no information at all on what the Professor had been doing for the last twenty years. Evidently Kurtowski was alive in an underground laboratory somewhere.

Again, Vernor was tempted to try to join the Angels, but again his caution held him back. He was twenty-three. He might have spent the rest of his life in the library, preparing for an ever-receding future, but one day Andy Silver came to see him.

# TWO
# the happy cloak

**M**ost days the library was practically deserted. There would be a few people viewing infocubes in the small Hollownests around the first-floor lounge, and maybe a couple of people punching questions into the Information Terminal in the middle of the lounge; but Vernor usually had the upstairs to himself. It was here that they had the microfiches with the marvelous access and viewing system that made picking out and reading any book in existence no harder than reaching across a desk and turning a dial.

On an average day the only interruptions were from the cleaning robots. Occasionally someone might wander up and spend a few hours at one of the other viewers, but never before had someone come up to read over Vernor's shoulder. He turned in some annoyance and immediately recognized Andy Silver's ethereally cynical face.

"I've been thinking about you a lot," Vernor said, standing up. "You got any of that dope?"

Silver smiled at and through Vernor, "Vernor Maxwell," he said, "I came out here to find you."

"How'd you know I was here?" Vernor asked.

"The Professor told me. He keeps an eye out for people who read his stuff and ask about him. You want dope? You'll get it, don't worry." Silver felt in his pockets, "You got any seeweed on you?"

"Sure," Vernor said. "This is where I live. Just a minute." Vernor kept most of his possessions wedged under a couch's cushions. He lifted up a cushion and took out a stick of weed. "This is really good shit," he said. "I grew this under ultraviolet light."

"High energy," Silver said, lighting up and inhaling deeply. "You want to be an Angel, Vernor?" Just like that.

"I don't know if I can handle it," Vernor confessed, "That's why I haven't come in for a test."

"It's not as hard as you think," Silver said. "It's just the squares who can't handle it. You know how to trip, right?" He passed the reefer to Vernor.

"Yeah." Deep drag.

"Most people don't. I mean, hardly *any*one does. They know how to get wasted, or how to get high, or how to feel good, or how to pick the nose, or bleed on the floor, or booga-loo, or WHAT," Silver suddenly shouted, "WHAT AM I TALKING ABOUT?"

"Tripping," Vernor shot back.

Andy Silver chuckled through his smile. "You'll be okay. Let's take a walk."

They finished the seeweed on the way out to the street. It was good stuff, and being with Andy Silver provided an incredible contact high as well.

They walked a few blocks in the gathering dusk. Vernor

wanted to ask about the Professor Kurtowski, but the stoned silence was too comfortable to break. As they drew abreast of a staircase down through the sidewalk to the walk-tubes, Silver suddenly pressed something into Vernor's hand.

"Take this," he said. "It'll help you study," and then he was gone.

It was a small pill the size of an aspirin tablet. "ZZ-74," Vernor murmured reverently, and swallowed it.

He spent the rest of the night wandering the streets of Dreamtown. ZZ-74 was different . . . a new place. Around dawn, he returned to the library. It was locked for the night and he sat on the steps. What had happened during the last twelve hours? He recalled a phrase from a book called *Ascent to the Absolute*, ". . . of some of our packed thoughts it is as proper to say that they are very rich in distinct items as that they are wholly void of any distinct items at all . . ." What *was* ZZ-74? What was anything? That night, Vernor Maxwell became an Angel.

He spent the next day recuperating, and the day after he went in for his test. The Angels' operation had expanded to include a whole building, christened the Experimental Metaphysics, or em, building. It was not that a building's worth of technicians, secretaries, data analysts, standing committees, etc. was in any way necessary for the Angels' activities. It was just that so little was happening in the Drones' lives that they came hungrily buzzing around when there was a scent of real action.

At the em building, Vernor found a few other young Dreamers applying for membership in the Angels. Only one besides Vernor made it through the initial screening to be sent upstairs for a machine test. She was a pretty woman, and they rode up in the elevator together.

Vernor looked at her hungrily. They might both be dead in an hour. Sadly he compared their healthy young bodies, imagining the delights they could give each other. He was practically a virgin . . . he'd had his share of playful romps, but never a real liaison. He could make out the shape of her privates through the taut fabric of her pants. He moaned softly.

"Are you scared?" she asked suddenly. He raised his eyes from her crotch to her face. She was looking at him pleasantly, openly. "Because I am," she continued. "I'm not going to do it. I just decided."

"You're not . . ." he said, breaking the eye contact. "Oh, I'll do it. I met Andy Silver. He told me it would be easy for me." As he said these words they sounded false to him. At the advice of a madman he was going to plug his brain into the world's biggest machine?

"You met him?" The girl was interested, "What was he like?" The elevator was coasting to a stop.

"Weird. We got high and he gave me some zz-74." Saying the name of the magic drug worked like a charm on Vernor. Suddenly his confidence returned and he stepped from the elevator. "What's your name?" he said, holding the door.

"Alice," she said. "Alice Gajary."

He hesitated a moment longer. "And you're going back down?" She nodded. "If I make it can I come see you tonight?" She nodded again, and as the elevator doors closed she told him her address.

"32 Mao Street. Come for supper." And then she was gone.

A white-coated lady beckoned to Vernor and he followed the coat down the hall. The guide nodded at the various rooms they passed, explaining their functions. The artificial intelligence laboratory caught his eye, it was a whole roomful of marvelous looking technical devices. A man was sitting at a bench cutting a thick sheet of plastic with a heavy-duty industrial laser. Safety precautions seemed to be minimal here.

"And here," the guide was suddenly saying, "is where you . . . drool or fly." She opened a door and he entered to find two men waiting for him. One was a technician bent over a bank of dials, the other was a Japanese man wearing street clothes.

"My name is Moto-O," the latter said, stepping forward. "I am newest Angel and will supervise test." No smiles.

Vernor sat down in the chair they indicated. He started violently when the technician slipped a plug into the socket at the base of his skull, but Moto-O gestured reassuringly.

"Phizwhiz not turned on, Mr. Maxwell," Moto-O said. "You decide when." He indicated a rheostat dial on the panel in front of Vernor. "You make it to five, and you are Angel," he added, finally smiling.

The switch was a dial with the numbers zero through five on it. At present it was set at zero. Moto-O and the technician moved away from Vernor, and he was alone with the machine. Clearly the idea was to inch up to five, hang on for a minute, and whip back to zero.

Cautiously, Vernor turned the dial just the tiniest bit towards one, and then, feeling only a slight tickle, jumped it to two. He closed his eyes to savor his impressions. "A garden of light," Andy had said, and that wasn't far wrong.

Patterns formed and dissolved faster than Vernor could objectify them. That is, he would *experience* a certain train of thought with its concomitant association blocks, but the whole mental structure would turn into a new one before he could step outside of it and *record* it. As yet, however, the thoughts did not feel much different from his ordinary thoughts, though it was hard to be sure. It felt pretty good, actually.

He felt light-headed, reckless. He reached out and turned the dial up to five with one motion. Only after they unplugged him ten minutes later did he have time to try to form a description of what full brain interlock with Phizwhiz felt like.

As he told Alice at supper that night, it was like suddenly having your brain become thousands of times larger. Our normal thoughts consist of association blocks woven together to form a network pattern which changes as time goes on. When Vernor was plugged into Phizwhiz, the association blocks became larger, and the networks more complex. He recalled, for instance, having thought fleetingly of his hand on the control switch. As soon as the concept *hand* formed in his mind, Phizwhiz had internally displayed every scrap of information in his memory banks related to the key-word *hand*. All the literary allusions to, all the physiological studies of, all the known uses for *hands* were simultaneously held in the Vernor-Phizwhiz joint consciousness. All this as well as images of all the paintings, photographs, X-rays, Hollows, etc. of *hands* which were stored in Phizwhiz's memory bank. And this was just a part of one association block involved in one thought network.

The thought networks were of such a fabulous richness and complexity that it would have been physically impossible to fit any of them into Vernor's unplugged brain. Once Moto-O disconnected him, they were gone.

"Wait," Vernor cried, "I was just about to get the whole picture." He had a feeling that some transcendent revelation had been cut short.

Moto-O laughed in delight, "You were almost gone to *be* whole picture. One more minute and . . . wearing the Happy Cloak."

Suddenly Vernor remembered that this had been a test. "I'm an Angel now?"

"Oh yes," Moto-O replied, "I welcome you." He shook Vernor's hand.

The technician looked up from a bank of dials and nodded at Vernor. "The system is definitely energized, Mr. Maxwell. You do good work."

"That's what I don't get," Alice asked after Vernor related the experience to her over the supper she had prepared. "If you have so much better associations and so much more complicated thoughts when you're plugged in to Phizwhiz, why does he even need *you*? I mean it's not like you're adding a whole lot of brain space to the machine."

"It's not my memory or switching circuits that Phizwhiz needs," Vernor responded. "It's my consciousness . . . my ability to discriminate. Inside Phizwhiz it's like a sea of information. The whole time I was in there I was picking out pieces and putting them together into patterns. It was sort of like listening to static until you hear voices."

"Can't Phizwhiz form patterns of his own?" Alice asked.

"Only the ones which follow logically from his initial program," Vernor explained, then added, "actually he can pick out *random* patterns as well. But he can't do what a person can do . . . put together thoughts which are neither so predictable as to be boring nor so random as to be nonsensical."

"So he just needs your good taste?" Alice was smiling warmly. "*I* taste pretty good, you know."

Vernor knelt by her chair and began kissing her open face.

# THREE
## alice swims

Vernor moved in with Alice and began working with the Angels. Once a week he would go in for brain interlock with Phizwhiz. The next few days would be spent in trying to remember what had happened, and then he would start preparing for the next session.

As far as Phizwhiz was concerned, no preparation on Vernor's part was necessary—all that was needed from Vernor was his ability to form thoughts. Vernor, however, liked to try to use the sessions to work on his math and science.

The first few times he went in to the em building, he had prepared a mental structure of facts and speculation, a perfectly built fire awaiting the kindling sparks of ZZ-74 and brain interlock. Since, however, he remembered so little of these mental conflagrations, Vernor's preparations became increasingly desultory.

At first he spent most of his extra time doing things with Alice ... going to museums, youth orgies, outdoor Hollows, or just wandering around the City ... but as the months wore on he began spending the larger part of his time getting high at the Angels' hang-out, Waxy's Travel Lounge.

One place Alice loved to go was to the City's Inquarium. On the six-month anniversary of their meeting, Vernor pulled himself together and took her there. Their relationship had begun slowly to erode, and it seemed important to have a good time on this outing.

They paid at the Inquarium's entrance and left their clothes in the dressing room. Vernor wore rented swim-fins, but Alice had her own custom-made fins, yellow with red stripes and long trailing edges.

"I want to look like a guppy," Alice explained, fastening yellow and red streamers to herself. Mesmerized, Vernor reached towards the streamers.

"No, *no*," Alice said, dancing away and flipping into the tank. Vernor jumped in after. The Inquarium was a huge tank, some thirty feet deep and three hundred feet square. The tank was filled with salt water and stocked with fish of every type and description. It was possible to rest on the bottom of the tank watching the fish and dallying with your mermaid, since breathing masks were bubbling at the ends of their hoses all over the tank's bottom.

Under the water Vernor looked around. His vision was clear, as he was wearing special full-eye contact lenses. The breathing masks were like a field of dandelions gone to seed, far below him. Alice was kicking down past a large grouper and through a school of parrot-fish. The streamers from her body flowed back like fins, luring Vernor closer, delicately tugging at her in a way that he longed to emulate.

Before he could catch up with her, down at the bottom with the air masks, he realized hadn't taken a big enough breath. He shot up to the surface, gasped a full lungful and dove again.

Without Alice nearby, Vernor paid more attention to the full tank's appearance. It was as if he had shrunk to a few inches in size and jumped into a twenty-gallon home aquarium. There were kelp plants the size of trees. Dolphins whizzed to and fro, filling Vernor's ears with their squeaks and clicks. Schools of smaller fish darted and wheeled like multi-celled organisms. A large, pug-nosed fish seemed rather too interested in Vernor's swim fins.

With a last mighty kick, he scared off the fish and reached the bottom. He grabbed a foaming air mask and pressed it to his face. Pure oxygen with perhaps a hint of nitrous oxide. Exhilarating! Hanging on to a convenient coral branch, Vernor looked around for Alice.

Soon he was rewarded with the sight of yellow and red swirls behind a nearby reef. He pushed off and swam over to find lovely Alice lazing there, her breasts floating, and a school of fishies darting in her lap. She took a hit from her air mask and passed it to Vernor, her lips parted in a slowly bubbling smile. He followed her streamers forward.

Passing the mask back and forth, and with fishies swarming between their legs, they had sex down there, the pleasure enhanced by nudges and occasional nips from the tiny fish. The bubbles from their breathing mingled to form a silver curtain around their heads. At the last instant, Alice pushed Vernor away and he came into the water, his sperm jelling into an opalescent, gauzy network.

They swam up, dressed and went out on the street again, Alice pausing to pick up something at the entrance desk.

"What's that?" Vernor asked.

"It's a Hollow infocube of us doing it down there," Alice giggled. "I wanted to have some nice pictures of us, so I phoned ahead to arrange it."

"And that's why you pulled back so I'd come in the water?" Vernor asked, "So that your grandchildren would know it wasn't a fake?"

"Oh, Vernor, don't be like that. I just felt like giving you a shove. For fun," She looked at him warmly. "We can watch it in bed tonight."

They walked along in comfortable silence for a few minutes, not a thought in their heads. Soon, however, Vernor felt the familiar boredom coming back. He wanted to consume.

"You want to get something to eat?" he asked Alice.

She smiled and shook her head.

"How about going over to Waxy's?" That would be good. Some weed and a few beers.

"And watch you get stoned out of your mind as usual? No thanks."

"Aw come on, Alice, I just want to see my friends."

"I'm your friend, aren't I?"

"Look, Alice, we've talked about this before. I can't spend my whole life with you." How he longed to be in the pleasant darkness of Waxy's. "Look, I just remembered, I told Mick I'd meet him to work on some new ideas." This was bullshit, and Alice could tell. Hopelessly, Vernor continued. "You better not wait up for me."

Alice stopped walking. "Again?" she asked angrily. "Why can't you and your addict friends do something serious? I thought you wanted to be a scientist, Vernor. But now you just get stoned and let that horrible machine suck out your energy. You think you're a genius, but geniuses *do* something with their lives."

This line of attack had become overly familiar to Vernor over the last few weeks. It was especially annoying to hear since he knew that what she was saying was basically true.

"What is matter? What is mind?" Alice said, mimicking Vernor. When he had started out as an Angel he had thought that his sessions with Phizwhiz would help him to answer these questions, and had often bragged about this to Alice.

He still discussed these questions with the other Angels, and there were times when it seemed that they had arrived at genuine answers . . . but the "answers" they found were always a little unsatisfying when he wasn't stoned in one way or another. Doing the actual hard grinding work necessary for really scientific investigations no longer seemed possible to Vernor, now that he was plugging in to Phizwhiz once a week. Why break your ass working out the field equations for a hypothetical energy configuration when you could plug in and do the problem in your head in seconds. The drawback of this procedure was that once you unplugged from the computer, you weren't likely to remember the specific mathematical solutions which you had obtained with the machine's aid. It was not merely that the solution was too complex to remember, it was that it would have been obtained so rapidly that it was never permanently fixed in the mind.

So Vernor had the feeling of great mental prowess without having anything concrete to show in the way of achievement. He knew that he wasn't really getting anywhere, with science, with philosophy, with Alice, and when she reminded him of this again on the street near the Inquarium it was too much to take.

"Go to hell, Alice," he said, wanting to stop as soon as he began. "I've had enough crap from you, you stupid bitch." Why was he saying this? He wanted to apologize, take it back, but already her lost face was miles away from him, untouchable. Her move.

"Goodbye, Vernor." She started to say something else, then choked back tears, gave him a terrible smile and hurried ahead.

"Alice," he was suddenly shouting, running to catch up. "Alice, I didn't mean that!"

She turned, all grief refined to bitterness. "You don't know what you're doing anymore, Vernor. I don't want to be part of it. It's too sad. You're not the same person." Again she hurried off, and this time Vernor watched her go. He looked at his watch. Five thirty. Might as well go over to Waxy's.

The last conversation with Alice played over and over in his mind as he walked. She was right, sure, but she wasn't an Angel, not even a head, really. He smoked a stick of weed on the way over, bringing his thoughts away from the past and into his surroundings.

Dreamtown. Nobody working, but everyone with a

little money in their pocket. Street action was picking up as the evening drew on. Dope dealers ambled along the sidewalks, unloading the night's supply. Hemispherical robots glided along the curbs cleaning up the day's refuse. There were homeshops selling tawdry pieces of plastic furniture equipped with small Hollowcasters to cover them with an image of luxury, restaurants selling Dreamfood molded and dyed to look like old style food, and stores selling pornographic Hollow infocubes. Illusions were the stock in trade.

Vernor stopped to watch a street magician, an intense man with a cable leading from his head socket to a Hollowcaster at his feet. The magician kept a constant play of images dancing in a ten-foot radius about him. Most were abstract . . . clouds and stripes of color . . . but some of the images were more realistic. Donald Duck paced glumly around the magician, wearing a trench into the ground while black smoke issued from his ears. Daisy Duck beaked softly between the magician's legs.

A fire-breathing lizard came scampering up to Vernor, rearing up on its hind legs to display a bright blue erection. As Vernor watched, the erection swelled and the lizard shrank . . . until the erection had turned into a large piggy bank.

The slit of the piggy bank moved and said, "Got a penny for the old guy?"

Unpleasantly surprised, Vernor kicked at the Hollow, but there was nothing really there to kick. His foot passed through the image and emerged covered with blood. Lightning bolts shot towards him from the magician's

head and a voice of thunder said, "Let's have that dona-
tion, buddy."

All of his bad feelings from the fight with Alice came well-
ing back up and he walked up to the magician, addressing
him directly. "You're fucking with an Angel, douchebag."

The magician grinned at Vernor, sizing him up. A red,
rubber douchebag appeared and swatted at Vernor's face.
"I can take you," the magician said. "Duel?"

Dreamer duels were not uncommon. The idea was something like plugging in to a girl's socket while you made love.
Only in this case the goal was not ecstatic union, but rather
the annihilation of your partner. The magician snapped a
cable into his neck and handed Vernor the free end.

Vernor snapped the plug into his socket and stood
glaring at the magician, who slowly dissolved along with
the rest of the street scene. Animals and energy patterns
came at him, clichés easily avoided and shunted aside. It
was nothing compared to plugging into Phizwhiz. Vernor
began flashing a series of images, connected in unusual
ways to form a pattern of unpleasant strangeness. The
corny lightning bolts and leaping tigers from the magician's brain began to look confused. Vernor stepped up
the assault. It was easy, too easy, to take his present mood
of despair and loneliness and project it out at this man; to
show him that everything was nothing.

Suddenly the circuit broke. The magician had
unplugged. He looked at Vernor with frightened eyes.
"You win, Angel." Vernor unplugged, nodded, and walked
on. At least he could do *something* right.

# waxy's travel lounge

Ten minutes later Vernor arrived at the Angels' hang-out, Waxy's Travel Lounge. It was early evening and the place was beginning to fill up.

There was a sculptured black plastic bar along the left wall. The area in front of the rear wall was occupied by a Hollowjuke, and there were booths along the right wall.

The Hollowjuke was running, and the image of a larg-er-than-life couple making love occupied the rear of the room. The Hollow couple were singing a muffled duet punctuated by a yas-yas chorus from four Hollow mas-sage robots busy hosing off the lovers.

The booths on the right seemed to be occupied. Noises of sex came from some, and over the door of some of the others you could see the bottles of intravenous feeding set-ups, dripping mixtures of sudocoke, synthoin, vita-mins, and glucose into the arms of those inside.

There was a group of Angels near the bar and Vernor walked over. An Angel called Oily Allie was describing her latest attempt to build a flying machine. Apparently she stole pieces of machinery from the factory where she worked, and reassembled them in her own mad scientist fashion. Vernor didn't know her too well, but tended to stay out of her way, as Allie was something of a practical joker.

As Vernor walked up, Oily Allie looked at him, shouted "Have a drink," and pitched the contents of a thermos she was holding in Vernor's direction.

It appeared to be a boiling liquid, and Vernor dove to the floor to avoid it. Strangely, however, the steaming liquid turned into a cloud of gas before it reached Vernor. As the gas diffused, the coals on the Angels' reefers brightened, and Vernor realized that it had been liquid oxygen.

"Man, you looked funny, scrambling around," Oily Allie said, helping Vernor up. "Let me buy you a hit of seenz." Allie punched the order into the bar robot and fed in the coins. The robot extended a tube towards Vernor and he put it in his nose, snorting up the synthetic cocaine. His adrenaline dissolved in a rush of well-being and he was finally able to return Oily Allie's grin. She was a muscular woman with dark, spiky hair, not overly clean.

"What's happening?" Vernor asked.

"Moto-O's been looking for you. He's over there." Allie pointed down the bar. Moto-O was sitting near a light, writing rapid precise symbols with his Rapidograph pen. Vernor thanked Allie for the seenz and walked over to Moto-O.

"Ah, Vernor," Moto-O said, looking up. "I have new idea for mechanical mind." Both of them were interested in the problem of how one might go about making a machine which is conscious.

The problem was challenging, since the Second Incompleteness Theorem, proved by Kurt Gödel in 1930, seems to say that no machine *can* be conscious, i.e. aware of its own existence. The reason is that the only way a machine can be aware of itself is to form an internal model of itself and look at the model . . . and it is impossible for *any*one, man or machine, to fully know himself.

To see why this might be so, try to become completely conscious of yourself and all your thoughts. Easy, you may say, no problem. But wait, did you include the act of examining your thoughts when you made your mental inventory of what's going on in your head? And once you tack that on, will you be able to include the act of tacking it on? And that inclusion?

The problem is that every attempt to fully map your inner landscape adds new features to it. The map has to include a picture of itself, which has to include a picture of itself, and so on forever towards the Royal Baking Powder vanishing point. No matter how fast you move your mental reference point, you're always a jump behind.

It's easy to see that a computer would run into the same type of problems when it tries to form a mental image of itself. But how is it, you may ask, that we humans do, after all, seem to have consciousness and self-awareness? It cannot come from internal modeling, so how does it arise? Well it's . . . easy to do, but hard to describe. Be Here Now's one slogan that sort of captures the idea, but that's not too helpful if you're interested in programming a machine. As a matter of fact, Gödel's *First* Incompleteness Theorem says that there *is* in fact no way to describe how it is that we do it.

Moto-O had spent a few years studying Zen, and he seemed to think that the answer to their problem was

contained in the principle of the Zen *koan*, an apparently
nonsensical problem (e.g. "What is the sound of one hand
clapping?) which beginners wrestle with in an effort to
break the shackles of rationality.

"Consciousness is paradox," Moto-O was saying now to
Vernor at Waxy's bar. "But we exist in paradox. I raise my
finger and all the world is there."

"I don't see how you plan to program this into Phizwhiz,
Moto-O," Vernor responded, sipping a beer.

"I plan to split Phizwhiz work-space into two parts
which monitor each other. First part will say 'This statement is false.' Other part tries to decide if statement is
true or false. First part will evaluate truth or falsity of
other part's decision. Infinite regress."

"'This statement is false'," Vernor mused. "If that's a true
statement than it's false. And if it's false, then it's true."

"Exactly. This trick is heart of Gödel's original proof."
Moto-O grinned and took a swallow of speed-tea.
"Phizwhiz need built in paradox like human to be alive."

"But won't he just reject the program after finding the
loop?" Vernor objected. "Won't he refuse to assimilate it?"

"Phizwhiz need firm master," Moto-O replied. "When
program enter, and before he can reject, I will administer
tripled operating voltage surge to him."

"Like Rinzai hitting the monks with his stick?" Vernor
asked, referring to the Zen master Moto-O had talked
about the most.

"Yes," he answered, "and more technical reason is voltage surge will cause memory banks to open so that loop
can be forced in."

"I don't know," Vernor said finally. "I doubt if Phizwhiz'll stand still for it, though I know that he does want someone to program a soul for him. Are you going to actually try it?"

Moto-O nodded vigorously. "Oh yeah. Tomorrow I go talk to Mr. Burke of Governor's Research Council. If they give approval I begin real work on technical aspects."

Vernor thought about Moto-O's ideas, to the extent that he could. What is this that I am? What if Moto-O really was successful . . . would they still need the Angels once Phizwhiz could think? His reveries were interrupted by the prick of a needle in his biceps. He turned around to see Mick Turner pocketing an empty syringe.

"It's just a shot away," Turner grinned.

Vernor rubbed the spot on his arm nervously. A tingling was spreading up towards his head. "What the fuck was that?" he asked, but Turner was already dancing across the room. Mick Turner had been the first person after Andy Silver to become an Angel. His scientific and philosophic learning was minimal, but he had probably survived more trips than any three Angels combined.

Mick's main concern in his Phizwhiz sessions was to disrupt the functioning of the mechanical brain . . . to freak it out of its program. Vernor, Moto-O and a few of the others were more concerned with using the sessions to advance the cause of science; but the avowed purpose of Andy Silver, Mick, and most of the others was to radically alter Phizwhiz's functioning.

Occasionally Mick treated people the same way. There was really no telling what he had shot Vernor up with. Vernor started across the room after him, but the roar of the drug hit him before he made it, and he stood rooted in the center of the room, twitching to the beat of the Hollowjuke.

It was an electronic number now, played by robots, squat machines with mechanical hands fingering dials on their chests. The rhythm shifted constantly, as Vernor's stimulated brain hungrily followed the sound's convolutions. He began to dance, and danced through the rest of the song and into the next. When one song ended the accompanying images would disappear, and a new set of Hollows would be beamed out by the Hollowjuke.

The image for the new song was two-dimensional, not that Vernor, in his state, could tell the difference. It was a classical recording, the Rolling Stones doing "Gimme Shelter." The surf music introduction seemed to last several minutes. Vernor was dancing hard. The wild power of the main part of the song came on and the room faded, the singer's voice fatalistic over the god-like and authoritative surge of the guitar. In the background, a girl was screaming, "It's just a shot away, shot away, shot away, shot away," the sound dwindling like someone falling off a cliff . . . Alice? Vernor danced harder, eyes open, eyes closed. The song drove to its conclusion, "It's just a kiss away, kiss away, kiss away, kiss away." A shot or a kiss?

The drug wore off as quickly as it had come on. He was looking into Mick Turner's face. "You're the craziest of us all," said Mick, "We need you."

Too disoriented to form a question about the last few minutes' events, Vernor followed Mick back to the bar. "Is Alice here?" he asked finally.

"I saw her a while ago," Mick said. "She gave me this for you." He handed Vernor a suitcase. His stuff. The Angels were all he had now. "You want to sleep at my place?" Mick was asking.

Vernor shook his head, "I'm going to move back to the library. Starting tomorrow I've got to get myself back together." He felt shaky and frightened. The shot or the kiss?

"Have you seen Andy?" Mick asked.

"No," Vernor answered. "It's been awhile. I thought he was staying with Professor Kurtowski."

"Yeah," Mick said, "but I was just over at Kurtowski's. He hasn't seen Andy in a week."

Moto-O had wandered over, "Last week I see Andy at em building," he put in. "He say he prepare for biggest trip."

Mick Turner shook his head slowly. "That's what I was thinking he did. We better go look for him."

"What do you mean?" Vernor said, looking from one to the other. "You think he took an over-dose?"

"No," Mick answered. "It's the machine, not the dope. Every time Andy was going a little farther into Phizwhiz. He had the idea that he could *stay* inside the machine and take over . . . live there as 'a stable energy configuration circulating freely among the memory banks and work spaces'!" He had said this last phrase in a sarcastically precise intonation, but the next sentence came straight from the heart. "He was getting tired of coming down."

"We must go to em building and look for him," said Moto-O.

The three of them hurried out and rode uptown in a robot taxi. The door of the em building was programmed to recognize the individual Angels' voiceprints, and it let them in. They hurried upstairs, checking all the places where Andy Silver might have installed a private hook-up to Phizwhiz. Finally they found it.

It was a spare room of the cybernetics lab. Vernor was the one who opened the door, and he saw Silver's body lying on the floor, a thick cable leading from his head to the panel of a Phizwhiz implementation. Apparently he had been plugged in for several days. His body was completely inert, and it seemed certain that he was dead.

Mick rushed forward to unplug his old friend, but to his amazement his hand went right through Silver's lifeless form. It seemed to be a ghost, no, a Hollow of Andy Silver. Suddenly the image moved to turn its face towards them, and it spoke, fading as they stood there.

"Tell them I was a martyr for the Revolution," the voice said. By the end of the sentence, the image of Andy Silver before them had dwindled up into the cable to Phizwhiz, leaving only a slowly dying chuckle behind.

# FIVE
## vision

Mick Turner took over as the head of the Angels. Silver had left him his stash of ZZ-74, and Turner seemed to know how to find the mysterious Professor Kurtowski to get more of the stuff whenever it was needed. Vernor was eager to be taken to see the great man, but Mick kept stalling on it.

It was hard to tell what had really happened to Andy Silver. They never found his body, so they couldn't be sure he was really dead—or that he had ever really existed. Some claimed that Silver had been a Hollow all along, a fantasy of Phizwhiz. It seemed more likely, however, that Andy was a person who was somehow alive inside Phizwhiz.

The evidence that he had survived assimilation was indirect. It just seemed that after Andy Silver's disappearance, Phizwhiz's behavior became more radical, more provocative. This could, of course, simply have been the cumulative effect of all the Angels' work; but some of Phizwhiz's aberrations seemed to have Andy's distinctive touch.

For instance, the next time the Governor made a speech, something "happened" to the sound track and it sounded like he was drunkenly asking the public at large to turn themselves in to be cooked down to oil for Phizwhiz.

Several days later the USISU newspaper printed the secret locations of Phizwhiz's main components along with detailed descriptions of their mechanized defense systems. Incredible things began appearing on the Hollows, for instance an animated cartoon serial based on the works of S. Clay Wilson, one of the depraved Zap artists of the mid-20th century.

But Vernor was not fully aware of these events. He had moved back into the library. Alice's last words to him still stung and he was spending less time getting stoned and more time working. He kept meaning to get back in touch with her, but he wanted to be able to impress her with some really solid new discovery when he came back.

He hardly ever went to Waxy's anymore, but kept in touch with the Angels through Mick Turner, who dropped in occasionally. Inspired by Vernor's industry, Mick even read part of *Geometry and Reality*, a book on curved space and the fourth dimension which Vernor pressed on him. But more and more, Vernor was alone with his ideas. He had finally worked his way out to the place where science shades into fiction.

He was getting deeply interested in determining the fundamental nature of matter. The conventional notion is that there is a sort of lower bound to the size of particles. You can break things down through the molecular, atomic, nuclear, and elementary particle levels ... but eventually you reach a dead end, where you have some final smallest particles, called perhaps quarks.

There is a certain difficulty with this conventional view that there is such a thing as a smallest particle: What are *these* particles made of? That is, when someone asks what a rock is made of, you can answer, "a cloud of molecules"; and if someone asks what a molecule is made of, you can answer, "a cloud of atoms"; but if there is nothing smaller than quarks, what *is* a quark made of?

Vernor had been toying with the idea of the infinite divisibility of matter. A quark would be a cloud of even smaller things, called, say, darks . . . and darks would be clouds of barks, and barks would be clouds of marks, and so on ad infinitum. In this situation, there would *be* no matter . . . for any particle you pointed to would turn out, on closer examination, to be mostly empty space with a few smaller particles floating in it . . . and each of these smaller particles would, again, be a flock of still smaller particles floating in empty space . . . and so on. According to Vernor, an object, such as a book, would simply be a cloud of clouds of clouds of clouds of . . . nothing but pure structure.

Vernor reasoned further that if there was no limit to how *small* objects could be, then perhaps there was no limit to how *large* they could be. This would mean that the hierarchy; planet, solar system, star cluster, galaxy, group of galaxies . . . should continue ever upwards, ramifying out into an infinite universe.

Vernor had studied enough Cantorian set theory to be comfortable with infinity in the abstract, but there was something definitely unsettling about a doubly infinite universe. Was there no way to avoid these infinities without baldly claiming that there is nothing smaller than *this*, and nothing larger than *that*? The solution came to him one night when he had the great vision of his life.

After a good day's work, Vernor smoked a joint one evening and, moved to do something new, went out into the garden behind the library. There was a large tree there, and he was able to climb to its fork some twelve feet up by clinging to the grooves in the tree's bark and inching upwards. Once he was up in the first fork it was easy to move up the fatter of the two trunks to a comfortable perch some forty feet above the ground. He was barefoot and felt perfectly secure.

The reefer had, as usual, increased his depth perception, and his eyes feasted on the three-dimensionality of the branches' pattern. A fine rain was falling, so fine that it had not yet penetrated the tree's leaves. Set back from the City like this, in his leafy perch in the library garden, it was possible to listen to the incoming honks, roars, and clanks as a single sound, the sound of the City.

He noticed a hole in the tree some five feet above his head, and inched up, hugging the thick, smooth trunk. It was a bee-hive in there—a wild musky odor came out of the hole along with a steady, highly articulated "Z". A few bees walked around the lip of the hole, patrolling, but they were unalarmed by Vernor's arrival. He felt sure that they could feel his good vibes.

A soft breeze blew the misty rain in on him, and he slid back down to the crotch he'd been resting in. Closing his eyes, he began working on his head. There seem to be two ways in which to reach an experience of enlightenment

... one can either expand one's consciousness to include Everything, or annihilate it so as to experience Nothing.

Exceptionally, Vernor tried to do both at once.

On the one hand, he moved towards Everything by letting his feeling of spatial immediacy expand from his head to include his whole body, then the tree trunk and the bees, then the garden, the city and the night sky. He expanded his time awareness as well, to include the paths of the rain drops, his last few thoughts, his childhood, the tree's growth, and the turning of the galaxy.

On the other hand, he was also moving towards Nothing by ceasing to identify himself with any one part of space at all. He contracted his time awareness towards Nothing by letting go of more and more of his individual thoughts and sensations, constantly diminishing his mental busyness.

The overall image he had of this activity was of two spheres, one expanding outwards towards infinity, and the other contracting in towards zero. The large one grew by continually doubling its size, the smaller shrank by repeatedly halving its size ... and they seemed to be endlessly drawing apart. But with a sudden feeling of freedom and air Vernor had the conviction that the two spheres were on a direct collision course—that somehow the sphere expanding outwards and the sphere contracting inward would meet and merge at some attainable point where Zero was Infinity, where Nothing was Everything.

It was then that Vernor discovered the idea of Circular Scale. The next few days were spent trying to find mathematical or physical models of his vision—for he wished to fix the flash in an abstract, communicable structure—and he seemed to be getting somewhere. Circular Scale! This could be the big breakthrough he'd hoped for, the discovery that would show Alice he was more than a bum.

He was on the point of calling Alice, but then it was time to go in for his weekly session with Phizwhiz. Vernor went with mixed feelings. On the one hand, with instant access to all of the scientific research ever done, and with the ability to combine and manipulate arbitrarily complex patterns, it might be possible for him to develop his Circular Scale vision into a testable physical hypothesis in a matter of minutes. On the other hand, the personal effect of plugging in again would be to stop him from working on his own for several days, and could quite possibly extinguish the recently kindled creative fire in him.

As it turned out, Vernor was not to face this problem. When he walked into the em building he sensed that something was funny. Nobody seemed willing to look him in the eye. Nevertheless he went up to the machine/human interfacing room, and took a capsule of zz-74 out of his pocket preparatory to plugging in. Suddenly the room swarmed with loaches.

One of them snatched the pill out of Vernor's hand, and then cuffed the hand to his own. "Let's go, Mr. Maxwell," he said, pulling Vernor towards the door.

Another loach put his face near Vernor's. "We got you by the balls, super-brain. That stuff you're on happens to be illegal."

"The pill?" Vernor answered quickly, "That's just vitamins." If he just kept lying he could beat the rap. The loach had seized samples of zz-74 before but they'd never been able to get any of it to show up in the lab analyses. The belief among the Angels was that zz-74 was so powerful that an individual dose was too minute to be chemically detectable. Unless the Us had radically improved their lab technique, he was safe.

But the loach seemed to have read his mind. "We're not interested in the dope anyway, Maxwell. You're wanted for conspiring to overthrow the government." Vernor stared at him, confused. The loach continued, "It's gone far enough. We rounded up most of the others after the show last night."

"Show?" Vernor asked. "What happened?"

"Listen to him," one of the loaches exclaimed. "As if he didn't know." He turned to Vernor, "only thing I can't understand, Maxwell, is how you could be stupid enough to come in here today."

Vernor decided to keep quiet until he found out what was up. There was a crowd of Dreamer kids out in the street. Some of them had co-ax cable hanging from their sockets, and they held the free ends towards Vernor.

The fans gathered every afternoon to see the Angels who had plugged into Phizwhiz that day. It was hard to tell what they really wanted—action, good luck, zz-74, or just something to hope for. The existence of the Angels had done a great deal for the Dreamers' morale. Suddenly there was a real job which a Dreamer might aspire to, just as he or she was. It helped, of course, to have some scientific training by way of preparation for the high level of abstraction inside Phizwhiz . . . but some Angels, such as

Oily Allie, knew very little science and got by on an innate ability to bend without breaking.

Today the kids were more excited than usual. The loaches drew their stun-sticks, but the kids surged closer and closer. Quickly Vernor pulled his free hand out of his pocket and threw his supply of zz-74 to one of the wilder looking kids. A loach punched Vernor in the temple as the kid took off down the street, swallowing pills as he ran.

When he recovered from the blow, Vernor found himself in the back of a robot operated paddy wagon, gliding smoothly towards jail. He tried to figure it out. The Us needed the Angels. Or did they? Certainly the Angels had made life more interesting, and their assistance in helping Phizwhiz separate the information from the noise had led to a number of improvements in the Users' technology. But on the debit side, there was the increasingly sociopathic aspect of the changes the Angels had brought about in Phizwhiz.

Vernor looked at the loach handcuffed to him. "Do you guys have some kind of grudge against the Angels? I mean, haven't things been getting better ever since we started working with Phizwhiz?"

"At the beginning it was all right," the guard answered. "But after last night—"

"Everyone keeps talking about last night. What happened? I've been out of touch."

"Are you kidding me?" the loach answered. "You didn't hear about it? That's complete bullshit. You helped plan it."

Vernor sighed. "Just tell me your version anyway."

"It was the Hollows. It was all fake last night. It started out with the news showing a picture of the Governor being shot. Then some guy who was supposed to be Andy Silver came on and said that Phizwhiz was our enemy and we should go out and start wrecking machines. Some nuts believed it and started trying to tear down the microwave towers. A lot of equipment got smashed and a lot of people got hurt."

Vernor shook his head and sank back against the seat. He wished he had had a chance to take that pill—it would have made it so easy to float out of the police van, out of his body. It was getting dark and he saw several high-rise apartment buildings flash by. Everyone was watching the Hollows. You could look into each of the identical apartments, through the living-room and into the Hollownest; and in every apartment you saw the same Hollow scene, a policeman whipping a naked woman with a belt . . .

"Where are we going?" Vernor asked.

"We'll take you down to the station and book you," the guard answered. "You'll spend the night there, and tomorrow they'll probably ship you out to the prison. Over on the north side."

"What about a trial?"

The guard gave Vernor a funny look, "You'll get a trial."

Before he could ask any more questions they had pulled into the garage under the cop shop. The police van pulled into a stall and a garage door closed behind it. A loach was waiting for them. "Governor wants to see him," he said.

They rode the elevator up to the Governor's office on the top floor of the building. The office was not really as splendid as it should have been. Like everyone else, the Governor had cheap plastic furniture equipped with Hollowcasters to surround the tawdry reality with a sumptuous image. Unfortunately, the average Hollowcaster gave an image which was about as true to life as a five-year-old color television set. Of course it was possible to appreciate these images on their own terms—to admire the swirling flecks of static, the fuzzed edges, the slight hum, the drifting colors—just possible.

The Governor was there in person. Apparently he took great pleasure in being the one to give Vernor the bad news. "The Angels are through," he said through his smile. "Us no longer needs your Youniqueness."

"So who's going to give Phizwhiz soul?" Vernor asked.

"Moto-O is," the Governor responded. "He came to us with a request for the equipment and computer time to *build* a soul for Phizwhiz. Us thinks he knows what he's doing. Right now, Moto-O is getting a nice trouble-free replacement for you all built."

The Governor looked at a list. "You're just about the last one, Maxwell. We got almost all the others when we raided Waxy's last night. Where were you anyway? Helping Turner and Silver screw up the Hollows?" He paused. "If you tell us where they're hiding, we might be able to give you special consideration . . ."

"I don't know what you're talking about," Vernor said. "Phizwhiz must have done the whole thing by himself."

The Governor laughed. "That's not what you all said when he started turning out fusion reactors. No, Phizwhiz can't do anything this exciting on his own. He needs help.

But now we're going to have that nice mechanical soul Moto-O's building."

"Hold it," Vernor cried. "How do you know Moto-O's idea is going to work? It might take him years to get the bugs worked out."

The Governor shrugged. "He's got six months. We've got him locked up in the em building lab. In six months he gets a plain cell like the rest of you." The Governor leaned towards Vernor. "I was going to wait till he was finished before jailing the Angels. Until last night we didn't really have much reason to arrest you. But you guys made it easy for us with your half-assed revolution." He leaned back, "We'll do fine without the Angels."

"Are you kidding?" Vernor protested. "The society's going to die with a stupid machine running it. And it's going to stay dead. Gödel's Incompleteness Theorem says that nobody, not even Moto-O, is able to build a mechanical soul."

"Googol's Unfinished Theorem? Sure, how long ago was that written? Moto-O's a sharp boy. Not a dope addict like the rest of you Angels. My money's on him. And if he's wrong . . ." The Governor seemed to feel a twinge of doubt, but then brushed it aside. "Don't worry about Us, Maxwell. Phizwhiz knows what's good for Us. Goodbye."

Two loaches grabbed Vernor by the upper arms and began marching him out. This was really happening. Desperate, Vernor shouted, "Governor, I've got a new idea. Circular Scale! You can't lock me up. I can take us to the stars!"

"Who cares," the Governor answered without looking up.

# SIX
# walk in, mambo out

The loaches took Vernor downstairs to the cop shop. Suddenly no one seemed very interested in him. He was just another body to process—to voiceprint and holograph. Before he knew it, he was alone in a cell. The other cells were mostly occupied by bums—drunks and junkies. Loud Muzak was playing as a rudimentary form of mind control.

Vernor had often romantically thought of himself as a criminal, but this was his first time in jail. Initially he felt a sort of pride at this outward and visible sign of his differentness, but soon his mood switched to one of shame and anger. The other prisoners were noisy and the Muzak and lights were left on all night.

"I don't really belong here," thought Vernor as he struggled for sleep, "I'm not like these people." And, more strongly than that, "Why didn't I call Alice?"

In the morning he was handcuffed and sent to the security prison in the northern part of the City. He was the only prisoner whose offense was serious enough to warrant this; and his relief at being away from the others' constant talk of matches and cigarettes soon turned to a terrible feeling of isolation.

The security prison was totally automated. The robot-operated paddy wagon drove in, and a door closed and locked behind it. The van opened and Vernor exited to follow a Hollow of a guard through a series of automatically operated doors. Soon he was in a small cell thirty floors above street level. It was with a feeling of great relief that Vernor discovered that he had a cell-mate, a middle-aged conman.

"They're putting a goddamn Dreamer up here with me now," the man observed, noticing Vernor's socket. "Whadja do, kiddo, this floor's reserved for the hardened criminal types like yers truly." The man smiled and rummaged under his bed. "Got my picture in the paper, I did. Here." He handed a yellowing scrap of plastic to Vernor.

It was a clipping from usisu, the national daily newspaper. Vernor had hardly ever seen the paper. When he read, it was science or philosophy, and when he wasn't reading he was usually around people who got all their information from the Hollows. A small picture of his cell-mate was captioned, "Bernard 'Boingy' Baxter," and the accompanying article was headlined "Hollow Con No Wallet."

"I had the sweetest number," Boingy reminisced, "I'd put on this special suit that made me look like a Hollow. You know, it was kind of fuzzy and shiny and had little sparkles all over it. I'd get all cleaned up and then start beating on some Drone's door. Guy'd come out, usually drunk or strung out: 'Huh?' 'Greetings, Citizen!' I'd say. 'I'm a secret Hollow sent here with an important message for you from the President himself.' And the guy is, you know, looking around, and I'd say, 'Long distance Hollowcast from the Pentagon, friend, touch me if you don't believe it.' And I'd hold out my left hand, only, and this was the pisser, it wasn't my real left hand, it was a Hollow of my left hand. My real left hand would be up my sleeve holding a little Hollowcaster." Boingy paused, and Vernor nodded.

"So the Drone feels the Hollow hand and it seems all right and then I ask him to show me some I.D. so I know it's really him. And he gets out his wallet . . . and then I'd make my move."

"You mean you'd grab the wallet and run?" Vernor asked.

Boingy looked shocked, "I'm a *con*man, not a mugger. No, I'd just look real officious and say, 'Let me examine your money, Citizen. We're searching for counterfeit.'"

"And they'd give it to you?"

"Man, I was from the *government*. By the time they stopped to wonder how a Hollow was able to actually *touch* their money and put it in his pocket I'd be gone. Boing." He burst into laughter, almost certainly genuine, though he kept a sharp eye on Vernor's reaction. Vernor laughed.

"I'll probably win my fucking trial," Boingy continued, wiping his eyes, "I mean I didn't threaten them or promise them anything. Just 'Let's have the money.'" He sighed and shook his head, "People are funny." He stopped and looked out the window, sinking back into the unfunniness of his present situation.

"Well," Vernor said finally, "I was an Angel, but now I'm busted. I guess this is part of the trip."

The jail was automated in order to avoid any problems with bribed or kidnapped guards. The blank cell door never opened. Food came out of a spigot over the toilet, just like back in Dreamtown. In Dreamtown the stuff that came out three times a day had been different colors, but in the prison it was always gray. A gray paste—slightly salty, slightly sweet, a little starch, a little meat. "Sort of looks like shit, oozin' out by the toilet like that," Boingy observed at each mealtime, until Vernor attacked him with his fists.

But things reached a balance between them, and Vernor settled in after a few weeks. He thought about Alice all the time. He began to wonder if he wasn't better off without all the dope . . . when he wasn't wondering how to get some. One seeweed seed was all it would take. God knows he had enough piss to grow it in. But he didn't have that one seed . . . so he returned to his science work.

Vernor had told the Governor that he could get them to the stars. How? It was, to say the least, a little hazy. He began keeping a journal of his fragmented ideas and his daily attempts to piece them together into an answer.

Weeks turned into months. Vernor and Boingy had no contact with the outside world. Occasionally a Hollow of a guard would appear in their cell and give them instructions. Once a Hollow lawyer came to see Vernor, but he was not a great deal of help, as all he did was deliver a canned speech about how important Vernor's case was to him. Generally, Boingy explained, once you went into the security prison you could expect to go to court after several years, with a good chance of dismissal or suspended sentence at that time.

"I been in here three years," Boingy said, "and the only other person I've seen was the guy before you. They took him out one day and he never came back."

"How did they take him out, when there's nobody here but prisoners?" Vernor asked.

"The door just swung open and a Hollow asked him to come on."

"Why didn't you go with him?"

"The Hollow told me not to," Boingy answered, looking embarrassed. "I shoulda, you're right, but it was the Governor himself. I was scared. They would've seen me."

Vernor determined that when Boingy's trial came he, Vernor, was leaving with him. Alice and the wonderful outside world were waiting for him. Hollows couldn't see, they were just moving pictures. Still, there was bound to be a checkpoint somewhere . . .

The next week a Hollow of the Governor appeared and the door swung open. The Governor's Hollow gave instructions.

"Please come with me, Citizen (zzzt)," there was a pause while a special sound file played, "Bernard Baxter (zzzt)." The standard spiel came back on, "All other prisoners remain in the cell."

Quickly Vernor slipped across the cell and fitted himself inside the Governor's Hollow. A holographic image is an interference pattern formed by two low-intensity electromagnetic fields. The effect is similar to the standing waves that appear in a river's mouth when the tide is running hard. There was no real danger in standing inside a Hollow, the two fields filled the surrounding area anyway, it was just that in the region of the image they were almost in phase with each other.

Standing inside the Governor's Hollow was like being

inside a glowing cloud. Now, if Vernor could just match his movements to those of the Governor's Hollow, he could walk out undetected . . . at least until they switched the Hollow off, but it stood to reason they'd leave it on until it had escorted Boingy to the courtroom.

The months of clean living paid off. Vernor's synchronization was such that it felt more as if the Hollow were moving with him than vice-versa.

Without incident, they proceeded out of the cell and down the hall to an elevator. The whole time the Governor was talking—about democracy, fair trials, repentance and the new life, and public safety. "You will notice," the Hollow boomed as the elevator door closed behind them, "that there is a grate in the wall here. This elevator is also our gas chamber, for those clients whose lawyers waive trial. It is fortunate Citizen (zzzt) Bernard Baxter (zzzt) that your cell-mate did not accompany you. Trial is waived in such cases." The Governor and Vernor nodded to a wide-angle camera lens mounted in the wall.

"Oh, no sir," Boingy said, mopping his brow. "He wouldn't do a crazy thing like that."

The elevator door opened to reveal a courtroom. The Hollow lawyer was there, and sitting on the bench was a Hollow of the Governor. Funny they'd have *two* Hollows of him at the same time, Vernor thought . . . but they didn't. He was no longer concealed.

"It was his idea, your honor," Boingy shouted. "I didn't know he was inside you." But the Hollow on the bench was already spieling out its recorded speech. There was no camera in the courtroom.

"Citizen (zzzt) Bernard Baxter (zzzt) you have been sentenced to three years' confinement. It is only fitting that you should gladly make this reparation to Us, whose social fabric you have so grievously soiled. But Us is merciful as well as just. The sentence is suspended provided you sign this release form."

A piece of paper appeared on the Governor's bench. Boingy signed with a shaking hand. The Hollows disappeared, and a door to the street slid open. Trying not to run, Boingy and Vernor exited and started down the sidewalk.

"I don't get it," Vernor said. "Why did they let you off?"

"I already *been* here three years, Vernor. When you go in they decide how long to keep you, and when the time's over they give you the trial with a suspended sentence. This way there's no hassles with appeals and real lawyers. I don't think there *are* any real lawyers anymore, even."

"How long would they have kept me, do you think?"

"You would have found out at your trial." Boingy walked a few more steps in silence. "You better hope it was for a long time, because when it's time for your trial they're going to notice that you left early."

"Unless they notice sooner," Vernor added, glancing back towards the prison.

"Right," Boingy said shortly. "Right. And so, old pal, I bid you farewell. Good luck, and forget my name until you strike it rich." They shook hands and Boingy Baxter went off down a side street, bouncing on the balls of his feet.

"See you in paradise," Vernor shouted, and headed for the walktube entrance.

# SEVEN
# in mick's hands

Forty minutes later Vernor was in front of Waxy's. It was the first place the loach would look for him, but for some fucked-up reason it seemed more important to come here than to go straight to Alice. In any case, it would probably be at least a day before they noticed that he'd escaped.

He opened the door cautiously, but the place was just about empty. There was some odd music playing on the Hollowjuke, a recording so old that there was no visual track at all. ". . . just to raise me up a crop of dental floss . . ." a voice sang. Vernor looked around. There was only one person who listened to music like that.

Mick Turner was sitting at the bar, his hands cupped around a shot glass of synthesmack. Vernor walked up and greeted him effusively, but Turner seemed to be on the nod. His eyes were closed and he was rocking back and forth to the music. Vernor ordered a beer and a reefer. The place was so empty that Waxy himself was tending bar.

"Big bust?" Vernor inquired.

Waxy shook his head sadly. "They came in and got 'em

all. Except for him." He rolled his eyes in Turner's direction. "And he might as well be gone. Spends every day junked out of his mind and listening to the Zap." Last winter Mick had somehow talked Waxy into the routine of playing records from his fifty-three-album Frank Zappa collection afternoons. This seemed to be the only remaining tradition from the glory days of the Angels.

Waxy set the beer down in front of Vernor and handed him his reefer. His face brightened with a sudden hope, "Are *all* the boys getting out today?"

"No, no. I snuck out." Vernor lit his stick of weed and inhaled deeply. This was going to feel good. "How about Turner. How did *he* keep from getting busted? Haven't they come in here looking for him?"

"They did for awhile. They really wanted him, came in every day. But he has this trick. Look." Waxy pointed to Mick's shot glass.

The glass appeared strangely distorted, now shrunken, now swollen, warped in impossible curves which shifted with the slow twitching of Turner's skinny hands. Vernor looked at his joint, then at Waxy. Waxy shrugged. "He can do it to himself."

Do what? This was getting too mysterious. Vernor shook Mick's shoulder. "Hey, Mick! Come on, man. It's *Vernor*. I'm out of jail and we've fucking got to *do* something!" Still no response. Turner's lips were moving slowly, but only to the sounds of the record.

Vernor looked helplessly at Waxy, but the proprietor's sallow face was bent into a rare smile. "Spike him," he said, handing Vernor a loaded syringe. "On the house."

Vernor recalled the evening after he broke up with Alice. Turner had it coming to him. He plunged the needle into Mick's leg. As Vernor watched, his friend's nodding became less fluid, more stroboscopic. His eyelids snapped up like window shades, and his eyes began to focus—

"Loaches coming! Get down!" It was Waxy, who had stationed himself near the window. A blast of adrenalin pulsed in Vernor's skull, but before he could run he realized that this was part of Waxy's practical joke. He turned to tell Mick not to worry, but his friend had disappeared.

"Where'd he go?" Vernor asked, feeling unpleasantly confused.

Waxy was actually grinning. "He's right there. In his chair."

Vernor leaned over and looked. There were Turner's ectomorphic hands, all right. The hands were cupped together as if in prayer. Fine. But the rest of Mick Turner was nowhere to be seen.

"That's how he hides," Waxy explained happily. "He gets inside his hands."

Vernor felt like crying. It was weird enough just being out of prison after seven months, but . . . "Come on you guys," he pleaded. "Give me a break."

Waxy gave a sharp whistle, and the hands on Mick's chair parted, clam-like, to reveal a homunculus, a tiny, distorted Mick Turner. He seemed to be talking, but the voice was so high and quick—and the whole scene so unpleasant—that Vernor's brain couldn't pick out the words. As he watched, the hands seemed to massage the space between them and the tiny figure began to grow.

In a few seconds a very wired Mick Turner was squatting on the bar stool next to Vernor, with one hand beneath his feet and the other on the top of his head. Vernor dragged on his reefer, but it had gone out. On second thought, that seemed like a fortunate thing.

"Vernor Max. I was waiting for someone to break out." As he spoke, Mick was glancing around. In seconds he had made himself comfortable in the new situation. He removed the syringe from his leg—where Vernor, in his excitement, had left it—and he threw it at Waxy.

"Professor K. laid this on me," Mick said to Vernor, holding up his hands. There was a small disc of foil glued to the center of each palm. Wires ran up his arm and under his shirt from the discs. Apparently they were connected to some type of power unit which he wore under his coat. "Probably coulda used this to get some of you guys out, but then I figured anyone who deserved to be out would make it on their own."

"What is it?" Vernor asked.

"vfg," Mick said, suddenly cupping his hands around Vernor's head. The room around Vernor seemed to be growing, everything seemed to be growing, and his shoulders appeared to stretch out for a yard on each side. "Now your head's shrunk," Mick explained.

"Stop." Vernor gasped, though he felt no actual physical discomfort. "Turn it off."

Mick took his hands away and things snapped back to normal. "This is a portable model of Professor Kurtowski's Virtual Field Generator. vfg. You're the one who spent five years in the library. You must know what it is."

Vernor was incredulous. "The Virtual Field? Sure, his last paper was all about it. But I never thought he could build something that would actually generate it!"

"Yeah," Mick answered. "That's what he's been doing most of these last twenty years. Only now that he's got it, he doesn't know what to do with it. He wanted me to talk to Oily Allie about it, so he gave me this portable model. Only Allie got busted with the rest of them same day I got this thing."

Vernor didn't answer immediately. Something was nibbling at this mind. Circular Scale . . . could he *test* it with the VFG? Mick was still talking. The injection had certainly done its work. "So when the loach came busting in I decided to use this on myself. Actually I was going to blow myself up big and scare them, but I turned the dial wrong. Worked good, though, I must of hid from them twenty times the way you just saw."

"Isn't it bad for you?" Vernor interrupted. "I mean getting squashed up like that?"

"You saw how it felt when I shrank your head," Turner replied.

"It didn't feel like anything," Vernor admitted. "Really it felt more like everything else was growing than that my head was shrinking. Relativity."

Turner nodded. "Right. Just now the space inside my hands looked like a little bed to me. Outside you think there's not much space inside my hands, but the VFG stretches the space so there's all the room I need."

"Negatively curved space." Vernor mused.

"Right on," Mick answered. "*Geometry and Reality* by Dr. Alwin Bitter."

"That's the book I got you to read."

"Sure. That's how I knew this field wouldn't hurt me. It's just like I was a man painted on a sheet of rubber. You can fit the man into a tiny circle painted on the sheet if you just stretch the rubber inside the circle. Or shrink the rubber inside the man."

Vernor was beginning to remember more of Kurtowski's paper on the Virtual Field, "The Geometrodynamics of the Degenerate Tensor." The idea behind the Virtual Field was that it introduced a localized rescaling of the space and time coordinates, but the apparent forces could be renormalized away at any point—which was to say that the field could shrink, expand, or bend you without hurting. You shrank, but not by being crushed—all your atoms shrank at the same time, and none of your internal structure was strained or disturbed.

"The Geometrodynamics of the Degenerate Tensor" had ended with some fairly specific suggestions for the experimental investigation of the principles expounded, but by the time the paper came out, laboratory science had been banned in the Us. The dangers of uncontrolled scientific investigation had been deemed too great, and those who insisted on obtaining physical data were requested to send their experiment specifications to Phizwhiz, who would simulate the experiment and produce a set of data. The data Phizwhiz produced were obtained by straight calculation with a touch of randomization ... no actual physical measurements were made at all. The experimental data obtained in this way tended to conform rather nicely to one's expectations—unfortunately these were of no scientific value.

Determined to get a real test of his theory, Kurtowski had dropped underground, and was said to have constructed a large laboratory for himself somewhere in the Eastside. Andy Silver and Mick Turner were the only Angels who had met him, and Vernor gathered from their elliptical comments that the years of dedicated work had turned Kurtowski into something more than a guru.

"Mick," Vernor said, "you've got to take me to the lab." The VFG was what he needed to test his theory. "I had this idea in jail. Just before jail, actually. I call it Circular Scale. If we could get a big Virtual Field Generator I think we might be able to do something really amazing." His head swarmed with ideas.

"Just make sure it's *really* bizarre," Turner cautioned. "The Professor keeps telling me that he doesn't want his invention to be used as a tool of fascist oppression or beer-fart consumerism. Like, he didn't spend twenty years getting it together just to shrink turbines for shipping, or enlarge some lame dude's ass for his hemorrhoid examination. He was counting on Oily Allie to do something really dangerous with it. Like she says, Freedom *is* Danger."

"Did he already know that it's safe to use the VFG on people?" Vernor asked. "I mean, before he gave it to you?"

"On paper. He wasn't going to turn it on himself until someone else tried it, though. Freedom is also staying alive, y'know. For him anyway. I figure the reason he gave *me* the VFG was that if anyone was going to turn it on themselves it'd be me." The shot was wearing off and Mick was beginning to look less alert. "I was gonna go tell him about how things are going, but I've been in a bag.

Just couldn't get out of it, you know, waiting for something to turn up."

"Here I am," Vernor said.

Mick patted him on the shoulder. "It's good to see you." His speech was beginning to slur. "Hey, Waxy, gimme another bang before I fade."

Another injection and Turner was ready for a civilized evening. "I heard Moto-O was supposed to build Phizwhiz a soul to replace the Angels," he said. "Is that true?"

"Yeah," Vernor answered. "He was telling me about his idea a couple of weeks before the big bust. I don't think it worked, though. It's not crazy enough. There *might* be a way—"

"Well, where *is* that pimp," Turner interrupted. "It's thanks to him that the Angels are gone."

"He didn't know that was going to happen. Anyway he's probably in jail by now. He had until last month to finish the job . . . There hasn't been any big talk about a new Phizwhiz has there?"

Turner was feeling around in his pocket. "No, I don't think so. Look, as long as we're going to go to Kurtowski's lab tomorrow morning, we might as well use up what's left of the zz-74."

They split seven of the clear gelatin capsules—a hefty dose; although it proved not to be that easy to sort the zz-74's effect out from the rest of the evening's excitement.

The high point came when they played Zappa's classic cut, "Stink-Foot", with the VFG turned up to full warp. The room around them wagged and twisted like a melting plastic shoebox, but in full synchronization with the steady beat of the song.

The bent notes rippled in new but inevitable chord progressions, as Zappa's happy voice talked and sang, telling a story about a talking dog and a disbelieving man.

"You can't say that," objected the man in the song . . . and the dog responded, "I do it all the time. Ain't this boogie a mess?"

# EIGHT
## trips

Vernor slept upstairs at Waxy's. The room was equipped with a pornographic Hollowcaster. It was nice having a beautiful naked girl posing herself for him, right on his bed, but it would have been a lot nicer if she had been somewhat less ethereal. He was stoned enough to attempt mounting her, and he just about broke his cock with his first mighty thrust through her and into his mattress. His last thought was one of anger with himself for not yet having called Alice to patch things up.

The next morning he showered, dressed, and went downstairs for breakfast. "What's the menu today, Waxy?"

"Green. How do you want it?"

"With a glass of beer." Waxy filled a bowl with lumpy green paste from the wall-tap, and drew a glass of beer at the bar. Green was Vernor's favorite color Dreamfood. They called it Dreamfood because all the Dreamers ate it. It came free for anyone in Dreamtown. A different color-coded flavor for every meal. Green *tasted* like scrambled eggs with bits of toast and bacon. If you were going to eat it, you didn't ask what it *was*.

"What ever happened to Mick last night?" Vernor asked between mouthfuls.

Waxy jerked his head towards the closest booth. "He took a hit of Three-way and went in there to ride it out."

Vernor finished his breakfast and went over to the booth. Three-way was a particularly vicious combination of a stimulant, a depressant, and a hallucinogen—all highly synthetic. But Vernor was not prepared for the sight which greeted him when he opened the door of Turner's booth.

Mick's torso was bloated to twice it's normal size, his arms and legs were twisted at hideous, unnatural angles, and half of his head seemed to have withered. He looked like a painting by Francis Bacon.

Vernor watched with mounting horror as the torso began to quiver, jelly-like, and the ruined head turned slowly toward him, the normal half slowly shrinking to match the other half. Unbelievably the apple-like head spoke, "You look really fucked, Vernor." Of course! It was the VFG.

Vernor exhaled. "Please turn that thing off, Mick." A click and Turner zipped back to his usual shape.

"Never felt a thing," he remarked. "I just felt normal. It was everything else looked funny." Relativity . . . halve your size or double the size of everything except you . . . same difference. The Virtual Field was safe because it distorted space without inducing any curvature of the time axis. No time curvature meant no forces—just a nice safe rescaling of the size scales.

Once again, the fascination of weird science was drawing Vernor in. Turner breakfasted on a handful of leapers and they set off for the Eastside. The City was some thirty miles in diameter, but there was a rapid underground transportation system of moving sidewalks in the walktubes.

They took the stairs down to the Eastbound tube. There was a thirty-yard river of people flowing past, borne along by the small spinning rollers which made up the surface of the moving sidewalk. The people near the edges were moving no faster than a walk, so that it was possible to step on and off the moving sidewalk without difficulty. As you moved towards the center of the tube, however, the speed of the rollers gradually increased until you were doing about fifty miles per hour. Each roller was quite small, about an inch wide and a quarter inch in diameter, so the ride was smooth.

Kurtowski's laboratory was in the basement of a plastics factory, not far from the walktube exit which Mick and Vernor used. After Mick had pounded on the door and hollered for awhile, the door opened.

The Professor greeted them warmly. "You have good news?" he smiled. Mick shrank Vernor's head and then let it snap back to normal. "As I thought," Kurtowski observed. "A singularity-free diffeomorphism never hurt anyone." He turned to Vernor, "And you, pinhead, who are you?"

"Vernor Maxwell."

"Ah, ja, poor Andy talked about you once. You have studied my early work I think?"

Vernor nodded. "Mick was showing me that VFG. I sort of had a good idea for something to do with it." He felt nervous about telling his "good ideas" to so great a thinker.

"Let me show you around the lab, and then we'll talk."

Apparently the basement was no longer used by the automated factory above them. It was a huge room, with machines and workbenches scattered all around it; books everywhere, usually open to some valued passage; mounds of notes; used foodtubes and dirty clothes; and crates and crates of supplies for Professor Kurtowski and his machines.

An area near the far wall was the present nucleus. The density of books and supply crates increased as one approached it, and many cables led there. This was where Kurtowski was building his new large-size Virtual Field Generator.

"Ja," he said as they approached the main work area. "You are walking through my life here. This," he slapped a loaded workbench affectionately, "is where I tamed my little neutrinos. Over here," a panel of dials loomed over them, "was my listening machine." He stopped. "Listen, Vernor."

He handed Vernor a pair of earphones and began adjusting controls on the panel. A rapid, articulated sound chirped from the earphones. Vernor put them on.

There it was before him. But what was it? Laughable to force its magnificence into human words, human concepts . . . only float closer, closer, ahhhhh. Warmth and light enveloped him, and his body outline began a dissolve. He was a cloud. There was clear ether in between his particles . . . the particles were thoughts, and the space between his thoughts was black was white . . . no space, no thoughts, inside, outside—CLICK.

Someone had turned the phones off. The energy field in front of Vernor's eyes arranged itself into the basement of a plastics factory, into Mick Turner's face. Kurtowski explained, "That's the center of the galaxy, Vernor. The treble is the neutrino flux and the bass is the gravity waves. Pulsars and singularities on miscellaneous percussion." He smiled. "When I use it I generally set a timer to turn it off—"

"Put me down for a half hour," Mick said, taking the earphones. He tapped his head, "I'm down to summer reruns in here." The Professor tuned the machine in again and Turner sat down with a happy expression, his eyes open but not looking.

"I get a lot of *good ideas* listening to that," Kurtowski continued. "The problem is *remembering* them, eh?" He led Vernor on through the lab. "Controlling the virtual electron field's interaction with the neutrino flux was all I had to do to get my machine going. It was not so very hard once I realized that neutrinos don't exist."

"How do you mean?" Vernor asked.

"It's like the coast. There is a coast because there is land and ocean. Neutrinos are the coast between the regular particles and the tachyons. There is no *thing* you can point to and say, this is part of the coast. When you point, it is at land or at water. The neutrino flux is just . . . the erosion of regular particles by tachyons."

"Tachyons? The particles that go faster than light? I thought that since they're undetectable they don't really exist."

"Exist for who, Vernor?"

He didn't attempt an answer. They had left Mick Turner with the earphones and were now in the main work area. There were several lights, littered workbenches, and two roughly conical assemblages, similar in appearance and separated by about ten feet. Large wave guides led to the cones—apparently they were powered by radiation from the hulking transformer behind the workbench, which in turn received its power through thick bus bars leading up through the ceiling into the humming factory above.

Professor Kurtowski placed a chair in the space between the two parts of the Virtual Field Generator. On the chair he put a large clock with a second hand. "Watch closely," he said, turning on the machine.

The power switch was a dial. As the intensity of the field was turned up the chair began to be affected. The top of the chair's back was approximately level with the poles on the top of the VFG cones. The effects were strongest there. In a few seconds the back of the chair had shrunk to the size of a ping-pong paddle. The shrinking effect was weaker down by the chair's legs, so the whole chair seemed to taper towards its top. The floor under the legs bulged upwards, drawn by the shrinkage of space, and the VFG cones seemed to lean slightly towards the chair.

Kurtowski upped the power. Now the floor had bulged several feet, holding up a tiny chair which seemed to taper to a point. The cones were definitely leaning over.

Another power boost and the chair was all but invisible between the almost touching points of the severely distorted cones. "Now the other way," the Professor said, dialing back down to zero power. "Did you notice the clock?"

"Was it going faster?" Vernor asked. "It seemed like the smaller it got, the faster it went."

"Right, Vernor, conservation of perceived momentum, eh?" The Professor switched the polarity of the machine and began turning the power up again. Now the back of the chair was growing, the legs as well, but less drastically. The chair began to resemble a spike balanced on a depression in the floor. The cones leaned away, as if to make room, as the chair grew to some twenty feet in size.

Somehow the space between the VFG cones seemed to be taking up most of the basement, and the enormous chair was almost overhead. The second hand of the clock on the chair was crawling, its motion barely perceptible.

The change in time-scale surprised Vernor, but it was, after all, to be expected. Big things are always slower than little things—watch an elephant and a dog scratching themselves. Less metaphorically, when you shrink a watch, it's going to go faster if no angular momentum is to be lost. Professor Kurtowski turned the machine off.

"So what is it good for, Vernor? You have, I think, a project?"

Vernor collected his thoughts. "How small can you make something with the Virtual Field?"

"There is no obvious limit. At first I was afraid that a great enough shrinkage might initiate gravitational collapse to singularity, *but*, as the local densities of the objects in the field do not actually change, this problem does not arise." The Professor was in good form.

"So you think you could shrink forever?" Vernor asked.

"This is not entirely clear. Quantum mechanics seems

to say that when you've shrunk to a certain scale, you have to stop. But maybe they're wrong. Tell me what you have in mind."

This was it. The idea Vernor had been nursing ever since his vision in the tree came tumbling out. "Professor, I think that if you shrink something enough it gets as big as a galaxy. I think that just as going West long enough ends with coming back from the East, shrinking far enough below normal size ends with coming back from larger than normal size." Kurtowski looked interested and Vernor continued.

"The size scale extends out in both directions. Going down we have people, cells, molecules, atoms, elementary particles, and so on. Going up we have people, societies, planets, solar systems, star clusters, galaxies, groups of galaxies, etcetera. My idea is that maybe this size line is actually a huge circle. That is, maybe if you go three steps below electrons and three steps above clusters of galaxies you get the same thing. Usually the largest thing of all is called Universe, and Leibniz has called the smallest thing of all Monad. I suggest that Universe equals Monad. If you break anything down far enough, you'll find the whole Universe inside each of its particles." Vernor stopped and drew a breath.

"This is a *very* strange idea," Professor Kurtowski said, lighting a cigarette. He was so old-school that he was still into tobacco. "A *bizarre* idea. In this world of Circular Scale you have no matter; this is nice, yes?"

Vernor smiled. "The problem of matter *is* answered by the Circular Scale Theory. You take a rock and grind it into dust, grind the dust into atoms, smash the atoms into electrons and nucleons, break these into quarks and resonances, do it five more times and notice that what you're looking at is galaxies . . . which split into stars and planets, and the planets split into rocks . . . one of which is the *same rock you started with*. And you can go around again without ever encountering any solid matter—just form and structure."

"Ja, ja, very nice," Kurtowski smiled. "And you want to make the trip around the Circular Scale with my Virtual Field Generator, eh Vernor?"

Vernor gulped. "Actually, I was thinking more in terms of sending a piece of apparatus around. Like maybe a camera."

"If I can risk my beautiful machine, you can risk your neck, Mr. Maxwell. After all, Mick has determined that the field is not harmful. It should be relatively safe for you to make this trip." Kurtowski paused a moment. "But there are difficulties. There will be some serious difficulties."

Mick Turner, back from the galactic center, had been listening to the last part of their conversation. He grinned and slapped Vernor on the back. "The incredible shrinking man," he said.

# NINE
## ZZ-74

"Did you ever plug in with a girl, Mick?" Vernor asked Turner. They were dragging a heavy crate of synthequartz across Professor Kurtowski's laboratory floor. They had been living there for two weeks, helping to beef up and outfit the VFG for a trip through the place where zero equals infinity. Vernor couldn't decide if he wanted the machine to be ready for him or not. He liked this in-between time; for now he'd abandoned his dreams of Alice and had put normal life on hold.

"Sure," Turner drawled, "plenty of times. You get a piece of co-ax and run it from your socket to her socket and then you do it."

"Yeah, yeah," Vernor interrupted, "I know. But what's it *feel* like?"

"You *never* done that?" Turner asked in amazement.

"No, well, you know. I just never did. And now I may never get a chance."

Mick laughed and shook his head. "If you get into it it's kind of hard to get sorted out after you come. One time I wanted to say something afterwards and it came out of her mouth. The words." He grunted with effort as they rocked the box over a thick cable in its path. "Once I met a chick who had a dual amplifier. You both plugged into the amp and it mixed the signals and sent 'em back triple intensity. Actually there was four of us plugged into the amp. It had these long coil-spring co-axes. You get so merged—it's a drag coming down. Just being in one body again."

Kurtowski looked up as they approached him. "Tomorrow is the day, boys." Indeed the machine looked ready. They had constructed a tensegrity sphere of molybdenum tubing and nyxon cables. The two VFG cones had been rebuilt and attached to the inside of the sphere at its North and South poles, with the cone points almost touching at the sphere's center. There was a band of power units along the equator of the sphere, with a space left for a seat and a control panel. All that remained was to encase the sphere in a film of the strong, transparent synthequartz and it would be a functioning scale-ship.

The idea was that the virtual field would fill the sphere, causing the whole thing to shrink—sphere, VFG cones, passenger and all. The passenger, Vernor in this case, would be able to control the rate and the direction of the size change.

They set to work putting the coating of synthequartz on the framework of molybdenum and nyxon. The sphere was constructed to have a certain natural elasticity so that it would not crack under possible irregular pressures. The purpose of sealing Vernor off from the space around him was so that he could continue to breath when the sphere and its contents had shrunk to a size smaller than an oxygen molecule. Without the containing skin of syn-thequartz, the air which shrank along with Vernor might drift out of the field and expand to a non-usable size—after all, you can't breathe basketballs.

The Professor was in a talkative mood. "I'm very proud of you Vernor," he said. "This is the kind of thing I wanted to use my VFG for—not miniaturizing factories or shrinking doctors to clean out rich Users' arteries. Daring scientific research by a fellow initiate, *this* is worthy of my machine. And if you never return, if you never return, Mick and I will tell the world of your bold attempt to travel around Circular Scale."

"'At's right, man, you're right on," chimed in Turner.

"How long do you think it will take for me to complete the trip?" Vernor asked, hoping to change the subject.

"This is an extremely difficult question. We have the problem that we do not know how many scale levels there are. We do not know if you will move from one level to the next at a uniform rate. And, last, we have the difficulty that your time will run faster than ours when you are very small, and slower than ours when you, it is hoped, become very big. So I cannot tell you. Maybe ten minutes, maybe ten days, maybe ten billion years."

"Ten billion years," Vernor echoed. "Well. Look, if it feels like I'm not getting anywhere, I can always reverse the polarity and just expand back the way I came, can't I?"

"This can be done," Kurtowski agreed. "But you should not do it prematurely. Such a reversal, if carried out abruptly, could well produce a radiation field of a perhaps too great intensity."

"Perhaps too great," Vernor murmured. They were just about through attaching the panels of synthequartz. Tomorrow was the day. Maybe he should sneak out during the night. He was ashamed to have such a thought about the greatest adventure in history. But maybe? One thing, though, the loach was probably looking for him by now. The prison monitor must have noticed that there was no life in his old cell. They had probably sent up a robot doctor and found Vernor missing. How hard would they look for him? Pretty hard, he guessed. They would be looking for him in many ways: Simple surveillance by cameras and detectives; theoretical modeling of his projected behavior by Phizwhiz; and, most insidious of all, careful analysis of the data from the Dreamers' sleeping brains. If enough of them knew where he was, it would show up.

"Mick, did you tell anyone that we were coming out to the lab?"

"I don't know, man, that was weeks ago." Mick lit a stick of seeweed. The last panel was in place. "Look at that thing. You're really lucky to be the one in it tomorrow, Vernor." Turner laughed with just the faintest hint of a jeer. "Seriously, if you don't make it back, I'll get the Professor to send me after you." He passed the reefer to Kurtowski.

"I was just worrying about the police coming after me was all," Vernor said. "Cause if they're not I got a good mind to leave while you guys are sleeping tonight." They didn't answer and Vernor thought about it some more. It seemed certain that the loach would be after him. "Let's test the fucking thing a *little* bit at least." He drummed on the hull nervously. "Give me that reefer, Prof, I thought you didn't smoke anymore, anyway."

Kurtowski exhaled a lungful and handed the stick to Vernor, with a chuckle. "Smoke, no smoke, what's the difference. We exist. Once you're born the worst has already happened to you. You've been so worried about dying, but have you thought about what you'll do if your trip is . . . successful?"

"I don't know. Smash the government, I guess. Like that's the thing to do, isn't it?"

The others nodded. Sure. Smash the government. "That's what Andy wanted," Kurtowski said.

"Yeah," Mick put in. "Remember? He said, 'Just tell them I was a martyr for the Revolution.' You think he's still alive inside Phizwhiz?"

Nobody knew. They smoked in silence for a few minutes. Finally the Professor spoke up. "Did I ever tell you the way I discovered zz-74?" he said, turning to Mick.

"I been *waiting* for you to bring it up. You got any?" Turner was lolling against a panel of instruments, looking through the remaining drugs in his pockets. "I haven't had any in six months," he lied.

"Do I have any? Ja, that's the question. Do you know what it looks like?" Kurtowski asked Vernor. This was good seeweed. The air seemed to be made of a transparent substance more rigid and more clear than air. zz-74?

"Well, the stuff we were taking was usually a clear gelatin capsule. It was like there was either some gas or a very small pinch of powder inside."

Kurtowski smiled and shook his head. "No gas, no powder. Didn't you take it on the street once?"

"Yeah," Vernor said, remembering, "Sure. My first time. Andy gave it to me. It was a little white pill like an aspirin."

"Perhaps it *said* aspirin on it, no?" Kurtowski's smile broadened. What was he getting at? He continued the dialogue. "Why doesn't everyone take zz-74?"

"Because the Us can't get the formula to legalize it and go into production," Mick said. "God knows they'd like to."

Professor Kurtowski held out a closed hand and opened it. "This is zz-74" The hand was empty. As the truth hit him, Vernor felt the room around him recede. They were sitting in the light of a single lamp, magicians three, null and void. The wind of Eternity swept through him.

Mick reached out and took a pinch of air from the Professor's hand and snorted it. "A righteous hit, old man," he said, stretching out on his back.

Vernor popped a pinch of the air into his mouth. "The perfect drug cannot exist, lest it be dragged through the dirt by the infidel?" he questioned.

Kurtowski nodded. "Ja, I had this idea after watching what happened to LSD. You had squares taking it to improve their sex-life, even ad-men eating it for inspiration to sell cars—it was too accessible. These people would take it, but they would not see the sublime mystery, the white light, the All in Nothing . . . and then they would say that I lied when I said that LSD had showed these things to me. I began to doubt, and acid no longer worked for me. I went into the laboratory to create a better drug—I was a materialistic fool like the others. But one day, deeply absorbed in a synthesis, I dropped a beaker on the floor. As it shattered, so did my delusions and I saw the All in Nothing again. I was there and I had never left. To remember this moment I named it . . . zz-74. Later Andy had the idea of giving it to the people. Since there was nothing there, they could not destroy it."

Professor Kurtowski's voice seemed to come from somewhere inside Vernor's head. Immortality and freedom were man's birthright. zz-74. He lay down to enjoy the trip.

# part two

part two

# TEN
## escherichia coli

A shaft of sunlight slanting in through one of the laboratory's street-level windows woke Vernor. The other two were asleep on the floor near him, and the transparent globe of the scale-ship loomed over him. He was still high ... on what? He smiled as he realized, saying the word softly to himself, "Nothing." Had Kurtowski been putting them on? zz-74. Last night they had taken it in its purest form. He was still high.

Mick Turner was rubbing his large mouth. He sat up and looked at Vernor. There was nothing to say. They sat watching flecks of dust float in the shaft of sunlight; then got some food out of one of the crates near the door. When they came back to the scale-ship, Kurtowski had vanished.

"Let's do a test before I get in, Mick."

"Okay."

They rigged a timer switch to the control board to send the scale-ship down for three minutes, local time, and then back up to normal size. Professor Kurtowski appeared from behind a mound of electronic components and watched silently, finally saying, "Ja, ja, a little test is all right." He seemed no more eager to talk than they. Everything was poised in such beautiful clarity that one hesitated to muddy the vibe with opinions, desires, facts and figures.

Vernor clicked on the timer switch. The VFG cones began to hum. The field would build up to appreciable strength in about sixty seconds.

Suddenly there were feet pounding down the stairs to the basement laboratory. At the other end of the huge room a door was blasted open. It was the loach. The leader was yelling, "We see you, Maxwell! Don't make a move! You too, Kurtowski!"

Back to prison? Never to find out if Circular Scale worked? Isolation from his fellows? There was no decision to make. Vernor scrambled into the scale-ship as the hum of the VFG cones turned to a whine. The Professor was speaking rapidly to Mick Turner who then started towards the scale-ship as well.

The field was building up and already the objects in the laboratory seemed to be growing. Mick looked eight feet tall, and although he was running, his progress was slow and dream-like. The Professor had disappeared and the police were drawing closer.

As Turner drew nearer, the effects of the virtual field shrank him to something like Vernor's size. Vernor leaned out of the hatch and tried to pull him inside with one hand, while fumbling for the controls with the other.

The police had arrived at the main work area. The scale-ship had shrunken enough so that they looked twenty feet tall. Vernor was seized with an irrational fear that they would stomp on him. This was impossible, of course; as a foot approached the ship it would enter the field and shrink in size.

A last heave and Mick was in the ship. "Crank it up, Vernor!" he yelled with some enthusiasm. "I always wondered what atoms looked like."

Vernor had disconnected the timer switch and was, indeed, cranking it up. The laboratory looked like the Grand Canyon, and a loach near them loomed upwards like the Statue of Liberty. He did not appear inclined to approach any closer, but it certainly felt bad to have an enemy that big.

"Looks like they're scared to come after us," Turner observed. "While they're watching, the Professor can make his getaway."

"That's what he's going to try?"

"Yeah, he always knew the loach'd be here some day, so he set up some hideouts and secret exits for himself. He'll be okay. And we ought to be just about invisible pretty soon."

Vernor nodded, "Since the VFG cones are shrinking with us, I think the field isn't going to reach out and warp anything much. We *will* be invisible."

It was getting hard to see the things in Kurtowski's laboratory as distinct objects any more . . . there were just huge color areas with fuzzy edges. Diffraction effects surrounded sharp corners with pale rainbows, and it was hard to say exactly where the ceiling was. The scale-ship probably looked like a grain of sand to the police. One of them seemed to have decided to come after them, but his legs were moving as slowly as the hands of a clock. They were safe. Vernor was sitting in the pilot's seat in front of the control panel, and Mick was leaning against the base of the lower VFG cone, his legs stretched out on the lattice of molybdenum tubes and nyxon cables. "What happens next?" he asked.

"Pretty soon we're going to be at the cellular level. Not that we're likely to see any life . . . it's too dry here." The ship had settled into the floor a little bit. The small irregularities of what had seemed to be perfectly smooth plastic made the floor around them look like a gullied desert.

The scale-ship was slowly skidding down into one of these gullies. The cushioning effect of the field kept them from rolling, so it was easy to watch their progress. Although tiny in size, the scale-ship retained much of its original mass, and thus continued sliding through any obstacles that appeared. Vernor and Mick's time was speeded up so much that their progress appeared slow to them, although in absolute terms they were sliding quite rapidly.

The gully fed into a canyon like some gray and lifeless Alpine wasteland, high above the vegetation line. Sharp peaks were growing larger on both sides of them as they proceeded down the moraine. "You know," Vernor said, craning upwards. "I think I noticed this crack in the floor when we were building the ship. Look how fuzzy those mountains are getting—"

But suddenly the peaks disappeared. Small, moving forms swarmed around the scale-ship. "Mick," Vernor cried, "what's happening?"

"I thought you saw it coming. The lake at the bottom of the valley!"

The truth dawned on Vernor. They were underwater, beneath the surface of a minute "lake" filling the bottom of the crack they had slid into. The lighting was good and he could make out four or five distinct types of organisms in the water around them.

The darting forms which had originally attracted his attention were flagellates, small teardrop-shaped fellows who pulled themselves along by fitfully twirling the hair, or flagellum, which projected out from their pointed end. They were still considerably smaller than the ship and seemed to pose no threat.

There was, however, a large amoeba near the ship, and Vernor was glad to note that they were skidding away from it.

It was a threatening sight, gray and branched like a stilled explosion of mucus, swirling on the inside. If you looked closely you could actually make out the last four or five things it had eaten . . . fungi apparently. One of its pseudopods was hungrily bulging towards the scale-ship . . . but the amoeba was slow and they were still shrinking. Already they were no larger than the flagellates.

A new type of organism was now visible, a herd of capsules vibrating together on the floor ahead. Soon they would join them. They looked somehow familiar . . .

"Look out!" Mick cried suddenly. Something that looked like a hairy blimp was speeding purposefully towards them. The hairs on its surface seemed to be the size of a man's legs, and they were beating in vigorous pulses. There was a sort of pocket near the blimp's front end. The hairs filling the pocket were more flexible and seemed to be wildly agitated. You could make out the struggling forms of one of the flagellates and several of the capsules inside. Apparently this was its mouth, and it was bent on swallowing the scale-ship as a third course.

This was the first time Vernor had ever seen Mick Turner look uptight. "Shrink, Vernor, shrink!"

"No sweat, Mick, the field extends a little way outside our skin, remember? Anything that actually touches us has to shrink as much as we have ... and if that thing shrinks as much as we have then it sure as hell isn't going to swallow us—"

But then the blimp was upon them, its oral pouch a hairy dome above them. It struggled to touch them and Vernor tensed as it bulged towards them, even though, as the hairs came closer they dwindled in size.

Turner had regained his composure. "I guess you were right about that field protecting us," he drawled. "You think that thing is trying to *eat* us or maybe just give us a kiss?" Vernor grinned and relaxed a little.

Soon the ciliate protozoan gave up on them, and they continued sliding down the slope. A huge shining wall seemed to lie ahead of them. "What's that?" Mick asked. "It's so smooth."

Vernor shrugged. They'd find out soon enough. Right now they were in the midst of the herd of capsules. Bacteria. "These are shit germs, Mick," Vernor said, "technically known as Escherichia coli in honor of their discoverer, T. Escherich. Some honor, eh? It's not everyone who gets a strain of fecal bacteria named after him."

"How'd they get *here*? I mean, the lab wasn't *that* messy."

"I was just wondering that," Vernor said. "This water must have seeped up from a broken sewer line." The presence of these human symbiotes was somehow comforting. It was like being in a flock of sheep. The shining wall they had wondered about was coming closer, but before Vernor could comment on it, his attention was caught by a motion to their right.

One of the E. coli had exploded, disgorging something like a hundred smaller organisms from its inside.

"What are those?" Mick asked. "Baby shit germs?" But these new organisms certainly didn't look like the bacteria. Each of them had a large, faceted head, a shaft-like body and a few small hairs at the bottom of the shaft.

"Those are viruses," Vernor exclaimed. "T2 viruses, I believe. Watch them go after those poor bacteria." In fact several of the viruses were now descending on the nearest bacterium. Vernor and Mick watched the closest virus as it settled down, tail first, on the bacterium's skin. The little hairs at the end of the virus's shaft dug into the cell wall, and there was a pause while the virus punched a hole in the wall. Then the virus's shaft telescoped abruptly, and it ejaculated the contents of its head out through the shaft and into the E. coli's endoplasm. The virus's body was an empty husk on the bacterium's cell wall now; but the genetic material which had been sent into the cell proper was busy turning the cell into a virus factory. In twenty minutes the bacterium would rupture, and out would come a hundred more viruses.

Several of them seemed interested in the scale-ship, but now there was something more important happening.

Mick and Vernor had reached the shining wall they had noticed earlier. It bulged with their weight, and suddenly they popped through it, leaving viruses, bacteria, and protozoa behind. Once again they could see the lunar landscape of the floor's plastic, and a smooth dome rose high over their heads. They were inside a tiny air bubble stuck to the plastic beneath the water in a crack of Professor Kurtowski's laboratory floor.

# ELEVEN
# theory and practice

The skidding had stopped. The floor inside the bubble was level. They were still shrinking. The molecular level would be coming up soon.

"Did you pack any food?" Turner asked.

"Sure. You know where it is. Wait, I'm going to cut the power. I'm hungry too." Vernor turned down the power of the VFG field so that they would stop shrinking, but left it on high enough to prevent their size from drifting back up. If he cut the power completely they would instantly snap back to normal size. Conceivably such an abrupt change in the field structure would generate lethal synchrotron radiation. And, of course, even if they did survive the snap the police would be waiting up there. "What do you think the loach will do?" Vernor asked.

Turner was squeezing the contents of a food tube into his mouth. "Mmmpsf ul nnf a flm flm smpfmh," he responded, then elaborated. "They don't know that this is a *scale*-ship. So they don't realize we've got to come back to the same place we left. I figure they'll spend about a week in the lab ... ripping things off, taking notes for

Phizwhiz, making the place nice and safe, and waiting just in case we do come back. After a week they'll probably decide we're gone for good."

"But as long as we're down on this scale, our time is so much faster than theirs," Vernor replied. "We could starve to death or die of old age before the loach's exciting week in the mad professor's laboratory has become just another happy memory." Crankily, he seized a food tube. Aaahh-hhh, at least it was Green.

After eating, they lay around on the tensegrity lattice relaxing. Vernor was full and the air recycler made a low hum. As he gazed absently out through the synthequartz, his thoughts turned to sex.

It had been almost a year since he had gotten laid. For the zillionth time, he cursed himself for not having called Alice immediately after leaving the jail. The scale-ship's strange passage down to air beneath water had reminded him of the Inquarium. He'd made love there with sweet Alice.

"It's too sad. You're not the same person." Her last words to him echoed in his mind. She had been right, about him taking too much dope, but he *needed* it . . . or did he? In jail he hadn't really missed dope . . . in jail he'd been a different person, he'd had no expectations, no desires, no physical life at all. And getting out had been such a trip . . . these two weeks in the lab he'd never really come down, but now . . . now he was resting at the bottom of a shitty crack in the floor, surrounded by mile-high policemen who would be around for years of his time.

The only hope of escape was the slightly dubious possibility that scale is circular. And like an asshole he hadn't called Alice from Waxy's. He'd imagined he had lots of time. Alice, Dallas Alice. A slight moan escaped Vernor's lips. He slipped his hand into his pants and squeezed his aching cock.

"Need some help?" Mick asked. Vernor looked into Mick's outlaw face. The question was natural enough; many Dreamers were bi. Turner drew closer.

"No," said Vernor. "I'd rather just sneak and beat off when you're asleep." He paused. Why? "I'm scared you'd eat my brain."

"Eat your brain? Well, all right." Turner didn't seem to much care either way. "How do you shit in this thing?" he asked after a minute.

"Well, what do you *think*? You go outside with the E. coli."

"Won't the air rush out?"

Vernor shook his head. "The Professor said it wouldn't. The field should hold it in pretty well. The synthequartz is just to prevent the long-term diffusion of the air. If we didn't have it, most of the air would be gone in a couple of days."

Mick opened the hatch door. No whooosh. Kurtowski knew his field theory. The floor in the immediate area of the tensegrity sphere looked normal, as it was shrunk to the same scale as them. The floor sloped up on all sides of the ship, becoming rougher and more magnified with distance.

"Hey, Vernor," Mick shouted after a few minutes. "Give me those empty food tubes."

"What for?"

"I'm going to try and throw this thing out of the field. It'll shake up those one-celled hammond organisms and put some odor on the loach's shoe." Only Mick would have thought of that, Vernor mused, handing out the flattened food-tubes. Turner used them to pick up his turd and hurl it away from the scale-ship. As it receded from them it grew in size and seemed to slow down. Soon it was hanging in their field of vision like a slowly waxing brown moon. Before long it would break out of the air bubble and ooze up from the crack in the laboratory floor. Turner climbed back into the ship well pleased with himself.

"It'll be up to life-size in a few days of our time," said Vernor. "One minute loachal time. They'll never figure out where it came from. I'm glad you came along, Mick."

Mick examined the instrument panel. "How is this circular scale jive supposed to work? How can we get bigger by getting smaller?"

"You want the whole story?" asked Vernor.

"Tell me."

"Okay," said Vernor. "Basically the idea is that spacetime plus scale looks like a doughnut. Say you have a doughnut lying on the table in front of you. Now, if you laid a square of cardboard on top of the doughnut it would touch the doughnut in a circle." He looked at Mick for a response.

"Right. A circle on the top of the doughnut."

"Yeah. This circle is like made up of the points on the doughnut which are the highest," Vernor emphasized.

"Go on."

"Now if the points on this circle start sliding down into the hole, what happens to the circle?"

"It gets smaller," Turner replied.

"It gets smaller," Vernor agreed. "So we've got the circle staying horizontal and kind of sliding down into the doughnut hole, shrinking all the time. When is it the smallest?"

"When it goes right around the inside of the hole. When it's like the circle where your finger would touch if you stuck it in the hole."

"Good. Now dig, Mick, when the circle goes down below the hole it starts to grow."

"Yeah," Turner nodded.

"And when it goes down further to become the circle where the doughnut touches the table it's even bigger. And when it begins to crawl up the outside of the doughnut it gets bigger than it was to start with!"

"Man, what are you *talking* about with this doughnut story?" exclaimed Turner.

"Don't you see? We have 'getting smaller' turning into 'getting bigger' . . . continuously. By starting to shrink and then continuing in the same direction, the circle ends up growing bigger than it was when it started. And if it continues . . . if it continues in the same direction it shrinks on around to the starting position."

"Space-Time Do-Nuts on my mind," Mick said. "And that's supposed to be the universe or what?"

Vernor continued enthusiastically. "It's like each one of those circles is a size level. The first level is human level, then you shrink on down to the atomic level, the little circle around the hole. Next you get up to the level of the big universe when you hit the equator—the circle around the outside of the doughnut."

"What about that other human-sized level on the bottom of the do-nut?" Mick asked suddenly, "what about that?"

"Well, that *is* a difficulty with the doughnut model," Vernor admitted. "I feel that the doughnut model must be discarded at this point. The model's usefulness is simply to show that it's conceivable to have continued shrinkage turning into expansion. It might be better now to just draw a clock-face and call 12: human level, 2: cellular level, 5: sub-atomic, 7: galactic, 10: planetary, and back to 12: human level . . ." His voice trailed off.

"What happens at 6, Vernor?" Turner asked with an edge to his voice. "You got us into this and I'm not sure you know what the fuck you're talking about."

They sat in silence for a few minutes. What would the transition from the smallest monadic level to the largest universal level be like? Would it actually work?

Finally Vernor spoke, "I don't know, Mick. I guess I never thought it would actually get to the point where my theories had something to do with saving my personal ass." He sighed. "We might as well go further down."

# TWELVE
# real compared to what?

**V**ernor seated himself at the control panel and turned on the power. He'd taken a dump outside the ship, too, and before long the two turds were like misshapen twin planets beneath an unimaginably distant celestial sphere. The floor material continued to develop new complexities of structure; as they shrank, new peaks and mounds of the plastic rose around them.

Vernor stared at an outcropping near them. A few minutes ago, the edges of the formation had begun to vibrate, and now the whole thing was to be alive with color and motion . . . like a pile of flickering snakes. He slowed the rate of shrinkage to enjoy the spectacle.

They were now small enough to actually see the long chain-like molecules which composed the plastic floor of Professor Kurtowski's laboratory. The molecules were continually writhing and twisting, now joining together, now splitting in two.

It was hard to believe that the molecules were not alive. One in particular caught Vernor's attention. It was viciously attacking its fellows, seizing them by the middle and then snapping itself backwards to break them in half. It hesitated in its rhythmic task of destruction and seemed to be feeling for something in the air—like a caterpillar looking for its next leaf. Now it was moving towards them. Could it be after the scale-ship? Impossible, a molecule had no mind, but yet . . . perhaps their charge, polarization, or field pattern was capable of triggering a tropism.

The lighting had become spotty and varicolored. They were so small that the corpuscular nature of light was evident. When Vernor looked at the molecular landscape, he did not see by a uniform illumination . . . instead it looked rather like a badly turned Hollowcast.

"Why does it look so funny?" Mick asked. "Is it night-time already?"

"*That* question I can answer," Vernor replied. "For us to see something, a photon has to come from it to us. Now, any given atom in one of those molecules will bounce or shoot a photon in our direction only occasionally. And any given photon has only one fixed wavelength."

"I dig," Turner replied. "The flickering is because we're small enough to actually notice the different positions that the photons come from, and it's colored because each photon is a flash of just one color—" His voice changed suddenly, "*Look* at that fucker!"

The molecule which had caught Vernor's attention before was quite close now. Turner's outburst was prompted by the fact that this molecule had reared back and struck at them like a rattlesnake. Again, they were safe from assimilation, since before the molecule could actually reach them it would have to enter the vFG field

... which would, of course, shrink it down to nothing. Nevertheless, it was unsettling to have this flaring Chinese dragon flying towards them.

They continued shrinking, and soon it was difficult to make out the snakes which were the molecules of plastic. The flickering became more pronounced. It was like looking out into a crowd of people taking flash pictures in a darkened auditorium ... only each flash was a different brilliant color.

In general, an atom will emit photons of only one color most of the time, so it was possible to pick out the paths of some of the atoms in the swarm of light flashes around them. They moved in unpredictable zig-zags—like fireflies on an August night.

As they continued shrinking, three atoms came to dominate the visual field. The closest one gave off blue and occasional green flashes and was floating motionless in front of Vernor as he sat in the pilot's seat. The other two atoms were located directly above and directly below the transparent sphere of the scale-ship. These gave off red flashes and seemed to be vibrating towards and away from the blue flashing atom.

"H2O," Mick exclaimed. "Cool, cool water."

"Yeah," Vernor said. "That must be it. The angles look just right for those two reds to be hydrogens bound to a nice blue oxygen. This might be a stray water molecule from our breathing. We're inside a molecule." The blue-flashing oxygen atom was drawing closer as the steady, pulsating dance of the red-flashing hydrogen atoms continued. "Pretty soon we're not going to be able to see at all, though," Vernor concluded, as the flashes grew more infrequent.

"Why not?" Mick asked. "Why shouldn't we be able to see the electrons and the nucleus? They're there, we're still shrinking . . . what's the problem?"

"There's no way we can see them," Vernor said patiently. "For you to *see* something it has to send a signal to you. The smaller we get, the less likely it is that a photon will hit us. Once we're smaller than a photon I don't think it even *can* hit us." He thought for a minute, then continued. "But maybe—"

Turner finished his sentence for him, delightedly crying, "But maybe you're full of shit!" The darkness around them had filled with an even, milky luminosity. The actual particles of the oxygen atom were becoming visible!

"This is impossible," Vernor said as they drifted closer to the atom in front of them. It had now grown to the size of a weather balloon. The blue and green flashes had died out as he had predicted . . . they were so small that the chances of a photon from the atom hitting them were infinitesimal. Nevertheless, he could see the atom.

The electrons formed a sort of cloud or haze around the tiny nucleus, but a haze unlike any he had ever seen. If he glanced at the whole electron cloud there were no lumps, no individual electrons . . . merely the continuous probability distribution demanded by orthodox quantum mechanics. On the other hand, if he focused his whole attention on any limited region of the cloud, a small yellow ball would appear there . . . an electron orbiting the nucleus according to the laws of pre-quantum physics.

What he saw depended on what he tried to see! He turned to Mick, "What do you see? Do you see separate electrons or just a cloud?"

Turner gave him a strange look, "I see little yellow balls whizzing around a tiny pulsing thing in the middle. What kind of *cloud* you talking about?"

"The *electron* cloud, dammit. Electrons don't have both a position and a velocity. Heisenberg Uncertainty Principle. You *can't* see a particular electron at a particular spot moving in a definite direction with a definite speed. You just can't!" He broke off as an electron the size of a beach-ball glided serenely across his visual field.

Mick was silent for a minute, then spoke. "Yeah, I remember that Uncertainty stuff. It was on the Uncle Space-Head Show ... Tuesday mornings at nine. Yeah. Now that I remember that, I can't see the electrons. That's really weird, as soon as you reminded me it got all cloudy ... what *is* this?"

But Vernor had no answer. The electron cloud had now grown to the size of a cathedral. The glowing nucleus was a pearl of light in the center. The atom seemed to be moving towards them. As with the plastic molecule before, he had the strange illusion that the atom's behavior was purposeful, that it was moving towards them because it sensed their presence. Was everything they met going to try to *eat* them?

Vernor covered his eyes with his hands to think. How could the atom's appearance depend on what he expected to see? When he put the Uncertainty Principle out of his mind he saw a miniature solar system ... like now

... he watched the sixteen electrons circling around the oxygen nucleus. Mick and Vernor were so small now that their time-scale was on a par with that of the atom, so it was easy to watch the electrons as long as you believed in them ... there was one dropping down to a lower orbit ... a photon went wriggling away from this event. With a start Vernor realized that his hands were still over his eyes. He opened his mouth, but Mick was already talking.

"Vernor, I can see with my eyes closed! It's like when I took my first acid trip. I just *sense* where everything is ... *feel* it with my brain!" Without turning his head, Vernor could *see* that Mick was lying on the floor of the scale-ship with his eyes closed ... and he could easily hear him yell, "Oh, yes!" to the approaching nucleus.

Vernor observed the nucleus only superficially and grappled with the problem of how they could be seeing without their eyes. It must be some type of field acting directly on his brain, he reasoned. Conceivably a field could produce mental images ... the brain's memory storage was basically holographic, so perhaps the interference pattern between his memory field and some external field could produce these slightly hallucinatory images he was observing ... the nucleus seemed to glow approvingly ... but what kind of field would it be? The nuclear boson forces could not reach this far, the electromagnetic field was too coarse, so that left gravitation ... but, no, gravitational effects would be flattened out by the Virtual Field before they could reach him here. Suddenly the answer popped into his mind. "Probability amplitudes!" Vernor shouted. "The pure quantum field!"

"Man, stop trying to explain it," Mick said quietly. "Get loose while you still can. Look at it."

It was something to look at all right. The oxygen atom had grown to an immense size, and they were drifting in through the electron cloud. The specificity of their presence was introducing violent turbulence and instability in the atom. One minute they were in a swirling probability fog; the next, electrons were rumbling past them like trucks. Several electrons spiraled down into the nucleus, emitting a variety of smaller particles on the way.

Their progress through the electron shells was uneven; they proceeded in jumps, and each jump was accompanied by crashes and showers of sparks.

Suddenly they were through the electrons' domain and the bare nucleus blazed ahead of them, perhaps half the size of the scale-ship. It was growing rapidly as they drifted towards it. A deep rumbling filled their tensegrity sphere, and the smell of sulfur and burnt earth filled their nostrils. Vernor was not surprised . . . if the quantum mechanical probability field could act directly on the memory structure of his brain to produce visual images, there was no reason it couldn't produce the sounds and smells as well. Intellectually he was hardly surprised . . . but on the gut level he was as scared as he'd ever been.

The nucleus was a dusky red interspersed with patches of black and threads of glowing white. Its shape, although roughly spherical, was irregular and constantly changing. There was no doubt whatsoever in Vernor's mind that it knew they were there, and was waiting for them to get close enough for it to make its move. He was repelled at the thought of being sucked into the heart of the fantastically dense entity ahead of them. But surely the Virtual Field would protect them?

A terrible idea struck Vernor. Although the Virtual Field would prevent the nucleus from physically touching them, the spherical symmetry of the vfg field might produce a lens effect ... a lens magnifying and focusing the fantastically powerful nuclear strong forces upon the interior of the scale-ship. Of *course* the vfg field was acting as a lens, otherwise the intensity of the quantum probability field would have been too weak to affect their brains ... "Mick!" Vernor screamed. "We've got to stop!" He fumbled for the controls with thumb-fingered hands.

"Stay cool," Mick said reaching over Vernor's shoulder to turn down the power control. They stopped shrinking, and the nucleus stopped growing. It seemed to be hovering fifty yards from them, a balefully glowing eye as large as the scale-ship. There was some kind of tension growing in the back of Vernor's mind ...

Suddenly Vernor's hand shot out and turned the vfg field up to full. The impulse to turn the power up had come from his brain ... but what had put it there? The nucleus filled his mind as he clung to the controls, fending off Turner's efforts to turn the field back down.

The laboring vfg cones whined shrilly, and in seconds the scale-ship was a twentieth the size of the huge atomic nucleus looming ahead. The rumbling and the stench grew more intense, and suddenly a chain of sparks shot out from the nucleus and enveloped the scale-ship, inside and out.

Flames covered their bodies as Mick and Vernor watched the nucleus, now several hundred yards in diameter, pull them closer. A series of ghost particles bounced back and forth between the nucleus and the scale-ship—it was hard to say which were the ghosts and which was the scale-ship. A vortex formed and dug a hole in the protean surface of the nucleus. The scale-ship and its ghosts began to spin.

# THIRTEEN
# hyperspace

A twisted screaming—scream from each cell of whose? black noise, white flame, wet flesh rent—inside under where? screaming ever never-place, white skin burnt black, crushed taxi bleed—STOP! I me you?

Something shaking him. Was who? Screaming twisting black noise hush? "Vernor, can you see me?" You the was it? Black burn scream who. "VERNOR, come *on!*" Blacker spot talking scream. "ZZ-74, Vernor, *say* it. ZZ-74." See see heavenly door? Seize the empty floor?

"ZZ-74?" Vernor said. The charm worked. Vernor, he was Vernor Maxwell. And the other one? The blackness thinned out to reveal Mick Turner's stubbled face. "Are we all right, Mick?"

"Yeah, I think so," Turner said. "That rush kind of got on top of you. You should have been riding with it . . . *watching* the nucleus instead of thinking about it. It wasn't a lot worse than an overdose of Three-way. And the ship's okay."

Vernor looked around . . . the only light seemed to be from the scale-ship's cabin lights. "Where's the nucleus?" he asked.

"We're inside it," Turner replied. "You've been foaming at the mouth for a half hour and we've been shrinking the whole time."

"What did it look like? In the nucleus."

Turner shrugged. "You tell me."

On closer inspection, the blackness outside proved not to be total. There were a number of semi-transparent squiggles and blips around them, each so slightly colored as to be almost invisible. "Those could be quarks," Vernor stated, trying to impose order on this incredible reality they had entered.

"*Some* kind of doo-dad," Turner replied. "I think I saw the protons and neutrons a level back."

"What were they doing?" Vernor asked.

"Kept kind of bumping and smearing against each other. Looked like a sex thing. Yin yang. One of 'em came after us as usual, but we out-shrank it. We hit some haze then, and that turned out to be a cloud of these jellyfish."

The squiggles writhed around them, slowly expanding as the scale-ship continued to shrink. They looked like phosphenes, the internally produced patterns you see when you press on your closed eyes. The largest and closest squiggle was pale white. "What do you say we have some food," Vernor suggested.

Mick threw him a tube of green. "I already ate." As Vernor began squeezing the Dreamfood into his mouth, Mick continued. "We should've brought more food, you know. There's only another two days' worth left. How soon do you think this Monad equals Universe change is coming up?"

Vernor finished his food before answering. "Well . . . possibly never. It could be that matter is like an infinitely branching tree, with each particle splitting into smaller particles, and so on forever. If it's like that we could shrink forever and never stop seeing new things." They had drifted inside the large, pale white squiggle. The squiggle seemed to be a cloud of small, shiny balls. Vernor opened the hatch door and threw out his flattened food tube. It had GREEN printed on both sides.

They watched the food tube drift away, growing in size as it distanced itself from the VFG field. It was slowly tumbling end over end. "Look at that," Mick exclaimed suddenly, "the writing is backwards." Sure enough, the writing on the tube was alternating between **GREEN** and **ИƎƎЯ⅁**. Sometimes the writing was one way, and sometimes the other, and sometimes the tube seemed to disappear completely.

"The fourth dimension," Mick said after a pause. "The space out there has got to be four-dimensional. Hyperspace! Like in *Geometry and Reality*."

Vernor nodded. This book, which he had gotten Mick to read . . . how long ago? This book had stated that only in four-dimensional space is it possible for an ordinary object to turn into its own mirror-image. The argument for this proceeded by saying that four-dimensional space is to us as our ordinary space would be to that legendary race of two-dimensional beings known as Flatlanders. More precisely: The idea was that if you have, say, a flat cut-out of a left hand sliding around on a table, the only way to turn it into a cut-out of a right hand is to lift it off the flat table *into space* and turn it over. Since the food tube was effortlessly turning into its mirror-image and back again, it seemed to follow that it was rotating in four-dimensional *hyperspace*.

"Man, I'm going out there," Turner exclaimed, moving towards the hatch.

"Mick, I don't think—" Vernor started, but stopped hopelessly. He was still too dazed from his nuclear freak-out to assert himself. Passively he watched Mick open the hatch and swing his legs out. That had been the one flaw in Mick's enjoyment of *Geometry and Reality* before . . . "Where *is* this fourth dimension?" he had demanded of Vernor. "Let's get stoned and *go* there!" Vernor had explained at length that even if it existed, there was no possible way to leave our space and float out into hyper-space . . . but Mick had never quite believed him.

"Here goes!" Mick yelled, pushing himself off from the scale-ship. He drifted about five yards and disappeared.

Vernor racked his brain for the proper Flatland analogy . . . oh yeah, Mick was in a different space-like slice of hyperspace. He was also crazy. Just for openers, how was he ever going to get back? If he was lucky he might drift far enough away from the VFG field to grow back to normal size . . . but in which space? And what *were* those other spaces which the hyperspace was made of?

His brain gave up and he turned down the power of the VFG cones. No point shrinking any further until he saw if Mick was coming back. Crazy bastard. Vernor looked out through the synthequartz windows. The shiny little spheres were all around them. They had a strange way of changing size while he watched . . . sometimes even disappearing . . . but always their surfaces remained featureless. There was a whisper of sound behind him, and he turned.

What appeared to be a thin slice from the world's largest blood-sausage had appeared in the center of the scaleship. Vernor froze . . . attracted by curiosity, but repelled by fear . . . "Is that you, Mick? You don't look so good."

The shape of the slice gradually changed until finally what seemed to be an animated silhouette was floating in front of Vernor. It was like a thin, thin paper cut-out of a man, tinted all different shades . . . a strange shifting color pattern really . . . Suddenly Vernor realized that he was looking at an actual cross-section of Mick Turner. It was as if someone had, with a huge sharp razor, split Mick's front half from his back half and then shaved off one slice to wave at Vernor. Wearily Vernor fumbled for an explanation . . . he felt ripe for another freak-out . . . if only he could stop trying to explain, to understand.

The cross-section wavered slightly, and then Mick Turner was back in the scale-ship. He seemed all right except that he looked funny, crooked. He reached his left hand out towards Vernor reassuringly. "It's great out—" He was interrupted by a violent explosion in front of his face.

Vernor's gears suddenly meshed. "Go back!" he shouted. "You're backwards! You're made of antimatter now!" *That* was why Mick had looked funny; he had turned over in hyperspace and come back as his mirror-image. Which meant that each of his particles was a mirror-image particle: antimatter. When antimatter touches matter the two annihilate each other . . . combine and disappear leaving nothing but a burst of energy. The air from Mick's exhaled words had just annihilated the air in front of his face. Thank God he hadn't touched Vernor with that reassuring left hand.

It was hard to tell if Mick grasped all this before he disappeared again. Time went on. Vernor assumed that Mick was trying to make sure that he came back to the scale-ship's space unreversed. Several times Vernor thought he saw cross-sections of Mick outside the scale-ship . . . once two circles, as if of his legs . . . but still he did not return.

While he was waiting, Vernor turned to the real question. *How* had the space around them become four-dimensional? He thought of analogies. Suppose that Flatland had a thickness which was unnoticed by its citizens. Say that Flatland was like a sheet of paper and that the Flatlanders were normally like ink-blots which had soaked right through the paper. But if each ink-blot shrank enough, it would soon be a small black glob moving about inside the paper—which now would seem three-dimensional. Yes. That had to be it. The space we live in did have a slight fourth-dimensional hyper-thickness to it . . . just like a sheet of paper has a slight third-dimensional thickness . . . and now Vernor was so small that space's hyper-thickness was much greater than his size. So now there was a perceivable fourth dimension. Nice. Wasn't there something in one of Clifford's later papers—

Vernor's scientific reverie was interrupted by Mick's reappearance. This time Turner popped back right outside the scale-ship; and after cautiously spitting at the ship he climbed in. He looked the same as ever.

"So how was it, Mick? Did you see much?"

"Looked just like here ... with those Christmas balls everywhere. *You* looked gross ... like an anatomy chart. But what counted was how it *felt*."

"That extra degree of freedom felt all right, huh?" Vernor asked.

"It wasn't just *one* extra degree, baby. That's infinite dimensional space out there."

Vernor didn't feel like entertaining such a claim. "That's bullshit, Mick. Anyway there's no way you could tell the difference even between four-dimensional and five-dimensional space. Can a point tell a line from a plane?"

"Man, don't you see, all that is just intellectualizing. I was *out* there. *In* it. It's infinite dimensional. Go on and see. Go on." Mick seemed annoyed at Vernor's contradicting him and was actually pushing him towards the hatch.

"No," Vernor said. "I came here to travel around Circular Scale. I'm not going to risk fucking with higher dimensions."

Mick snorted in disgust, but he let Vernor go back to the controls. Vernor turned the VFG field back up and the spheres began growing. He looked at the closest one. Obviously they were going to have to get inside it. But it looked so smooth. It's surface appeared mirror-like; in fact he could make out their reflection.

It was funny about this shiny sphere, this Christmas ball, one instant it would be looming over them like an asteroid, and the next it would shrink back to the size of the scale-ship, or even smaller. By now, Vernor might have welcomed an attack from it, but the sphere seemed content to continue its solitary fluctuations.

The scale-ship was still shrinking, and the shiny balls were looking larger, but they showed no sign of breaking up into smaller particles. Could these spheres be the smallest possible particles ... totally dense, totally smooth? If that was the case, further shrinkage would reveal nothing.

Vernor cut the power. The closest sphere was almost touching them. He looked at Mick for help, but his friend seemed to be lost in thought ... perhaps of his "infinite dimensional" space. Vernor opened the hatch door and started throwing out pieces of the food crate. The hatch was on the opposite side of the ship from the giant Christmas ball, and he hoped to push into it by means of this crude jet propulsion. It seemed several times that they touched it, but only to slide off, or to have it shrink away from them. Disgusted, Vernor closed the hatch and lay down, panting with exhaustion.

"You know what that thing is, asshole?" Mick said finally.

"Is it an infinite dimensional sphere, Mick?"

"No. It's a hypersphere. Four-dimensional. I can tell from how it looked out there."

"Okay," Vernor said. "It's a hypersphere." He felt very tired.

"The *Universe* is a hypersphere, Vernor," Mick said quietly.

# god

**M**ick's statement was correct. The old Einstein conjecture that the space of our universe is actually curved around on itself to make a hypersphere had come back into favor. Vernor knew, every *child* knew, that the space of the universe was a hypersphere—just as he knew that the space of the Earth's surface was a sphere. But Vernor had not been prepared to actually see a hypersphere. He *couldn't* actually see it all at once, but he had been seeing it in installments as he observed the various-sized spheres in front of him. Just as a sphere is a stack of circles, a hypersphere consists of infinitely many spheres, joined to each other in some unimaginable fashion.

"Mick," Vernor said finally. "I'm ready to believe anything else you tell me if only those things out there are each the universe."

"If those are each . . ." Mick echoed. "How can each one of those different hyperspheres be the same universe?"

"They're shiny aren't they?" Vernor said. "I figure they're sort of reflections of each other. But that can wait. The real problem is how to get *inside* one of 'em."

"You thought throwing that shit out the hatch was going to push us into it?" Mick asked pityingly.

"You got any better ideas? Or should I bring on the analogies?"

Mick shook his head. "Let's just rest. Maybe it'll come *git* us. I think I could probably get *my*self in there, but I don't think there's anything I could do to maneuver the ship into the right position."

"Like making a disk stick to a sphere," Vernor mused. "We really should try—" he started, but broke off in a yawn. He was bone tired. They lay on the scale-ship's floor watching the fluctuating cross-section of the hypersphere.

"I bet it helps to get into it if you're already out of it," said Mick. He lit a stick of weed and passed it across to Vernor.

"Just a second," Vernor hissed a few minutes later. "There's something different out there. Moving towards us—up there." He pointed. There was, indeed, something approaching the scale-ship from above the hypersphere. It was irregularly shaped and seemed to be moving with a sort of beating motion.

"Oh, come back tomorrow," Mick exclaimed. "It's going to be something else trying to eat us." The object drew closer. It was shaped almost like a man, but there could hardly be people floating around here . . . smaller than an atom, larger than the universe. Strangely, the object did not shrink as it approached the scale-ship . . . could it penetrate their field and devour them?

Mick gave a sudden whoop, "Hey, Professor, we're in here!"

"But can't be," Vernor moaned. "But can't be!" Sure enough, it *was* Professor Kurtowski. Reaching the ship he climbed in the hatch, sat down in the pilot's chair, and beamed at them.

"I'm dreaming," he offered by way of explanation. "I often come here when I get uncoupled. I was never quite sure before that this place was . . . shall we say *real*?"

Vernor's mouth opened and closed silently, but the resilient Turner was not at a loss for words, "Professor, is that thing there the Universe?"

"Go on in. Maybe you'll find out." Kurtowski replied.

"That's the problem. We can't get in," Vernor said, finding his voice.

"It's something you do with your head. Keeping still. Go to sleep. Sleep. Sleep." Professor Kurtowski was fading, and then he was gone, but this occasioned no outcry, as the two passengers of the scale-ship had dozed off.

After all had been quiet on the ship for some time, the ever-shifting sphere drew closer and dwindled to point-size. To an observer on the scale-ship it would have appeared now that the hypersphere had disappeared, but it had only moved "under" the ship.

Immanuel Kant called space an "ineluctable modality" of human thought, but Mick and Vernor were far gone enough to prove him wrong. All barriers were down, and the hypersphere rose to assimilate them.

Vernor snapped awake. Such a strange dream . . . first Kurtowski, then Alice, and then . . . what? There was an expanding sphere of darkness in the scale-ship with them. A darkness marbled with streamers of light . . . growing towards him. The scream stuck in Vernor's throat as he realized that they were home free.

"The Professor was right," Mick remarked. Strange, had he had the same dream? But no dream could compare with what they were witnessing now—everything, everything at once.

They were in it, filling a tenth of it. "The All," Vernor said reverently. It was alive. It was alive and glad to see them. The Universe. What did it look like? What does a head of clover look like ... or a rock or a thumb or a moon or a microbe? Nothing's really any bigger than anything else on the Circular Scale. But still, but still, if you expect a lot, you see a lot. zz-74.

The patterns around Vernor told him everything there was to know. When later he tried to express his feelings during those minutes of total communication with the Universe, he could do no better than to quote Wittgenstein, "The solution of the problem of life is seen in the vanishing of the problem."

But soon this passed, as it always does, and Vernor was analyzing, differentiating, observing. They were surrounded by a three-dimensional network of light. Pulses of brightness traveled through the network, forking here, merging there. A minute ago these patterns had seemed to be part of him, invisible, but now he could only gape and wonder.

"God's brain." Mick said simply. That was it. And what thoughts were they watching, what had they left behind? The network region near them maintained an increased level of activity. It was still talking to, in, them ... but Vernor couldn't hear it anymore.

Jolts and trains of energy rippled through the paths around them, weaving back and forth, rising and falling. Out beyond this region Vernor could see more and more of "God's brain," but it didn't go on forever. In many places there seemed to be dark clouds, but even where it was clear there was a sort of glassy barrier out beyond it all—

"Mick, see way out past all the light?" No answer.

"Out past everything. Like a glass wall. You know what that is?"

"Nuh."

"That's us!" Vernor said, happy to one-up Mick on the subtleties of life in a hypersphere. "The space is so curved that we can see clear around it to the back of our heads. Or the back of the scale-ship, anyway."

Mick grunted and turned his full attention back to the universe itself. He seemed not to want to get sucked into the scientific frame of mind. He was right. Once again, Vernor let his attention drift out into the friendly being around them. He found himself praying.

"One size fits all," Mick said presently, and Vernor nodded agreement. On earth as it is in heaven. As above, so below.

But the zest for observation returned, and yet again Vernor sorted his Self out into subject and object, scientist and phenomenon.

They had been shrinking all this time, and the nodes at the intersections of the network had resolved themselves into clouds of bright particles darting around exceptionally bright central regions.

One of the nodes had come to dominate their visual field, and they could see now that matter was continually being ejected from the bright region at the center.

"That must be a white hole," Vernor remarked. "You know, the other end of a hyperspace tunnel which starts at a black hole. Matter falls in the black end and comes out the white end, all cleaned and simplified."

"Where are the black holes?" Mick asked, suddenly brought down. "I'm not too eager to get my matter cleaned."

"It's kind of hard to see them," Vernor answered. They were quiet for a few minutes. The shrinking was proceeding at a good rate and the node in front of them covered most of their visual field now.

"Where do you think the Milky Way is?" Mick asked.

"Well," Vernor replied, "we probably have to go down a few more levels to get to the galaxy level. I imagine it's going to end up being inside one of those bright spots . . . according to my theory we should contract right down into—"

There was something wrong. The light from the objects ahead of them was suddenly getting bluer, brighter. The brightened lights seemed to be rushing in on them faster than before. It was as if the whole universe was somehow hurrying around to get in front of them; leaving only a terrible, hungry darkness behind the scale-ship.

A deep humming from the ship's tensegrity sphere entered the range of audibility. An incredible force was pressing on them; the very air began to sputter, filled with an unheard of energy density.

Without saying anything, Mick and Vernor realized together that they were indeed being sucked into a black hole. There was no way that their Virtual Field could protect them from the real and unlimited forces which they would encounter deeper in this terrible whirlpool of spacetime.

There was only one possible means of escape, and Mick thought of it. He went quickly to the control panel and turned off the VFG field. If they were not yet past the black hole's lip, they might still snap back around the curve of Circular Scale to their original size and location.

For an instant there was a charged equilibrium between the expansive force of the suddenly released space of the scale-ship and the contracting force of the black hole's gravitational field. Then, with the sound of all of Frank Zappa's songs played at top volume at the same time, the last minute of their trip was over.

# FIFTEEN
## exits

**A**s it turned out, the police were still in Professor Kurtowski's lab. "How did you guys manage to disappear for a whole half hour like that?" they wanted to know.

"We did it with mirrors," Turner replied, carefully stepping over the turds near the ship.

Better in jail than inside a black hole, Vernor consoled himself as they were led off. He still wondered how they had escaped the lethal dose of synchrotron radiation which Kurtowski had predicted would arise if they suddenly cut off the vfg. Probably the fucking black hole had blotted it up. That had been no accidental collision, oh no, the bastard had probably come halfway around the Universe to get them. And up on this level a thing called a *society* wanted his ass. Same thing in the end. Same fucking thing.

"I want to see a lawyer," Vernor shouted as they were led to the back of the waiting police van. It was an automated van, and the joke sounded stupider than Vernor had intended. The loaches were not talkative. They seemed eager to dispose of Vernor and Mick. Probably they were eager to get back to the lab . . . that was dangerous, exciting . . . not routine like mailing two losers to the detention center.

The loaches sealed the time-lock on the door, the idling turbine geared up and engaged, and Vernor Maxwell and Mick Turner were on their programmed path to an automated jail. There was nothing to say.

They were about ten blocks from the Professor's laboratory when a sudden explosion rocked and overturned the police van. Steps ran closer, paused, then ran off. There was another, smaller, explosion which blew open the van's rear door. A horn started a steady blast of alarm.

Mick and Vernor hit the street at a run, following the sound of those footsteps. They caught a glimpse of a figure hurrying into an alley across the street. It was the spry Professor Kurtowski.

In the darkness of the alley, the three paused to catch their breath, and to pound one another with joy. It was impossible to talk over the noise of the smashed van's automatic alarm. Sirens were approaching from several directions. Kurtowski nodded and set off down the alley with a beckoning gesture.

The alley ended in a blind wall. Too high to climb, and solid except for a small flaw at the base of the wall.

"Through there," Kurtowski said loudly, with a note of humorous challenge. "We must pass through the needle's eye to enter paradise."

Man, if you say so, Vernor thought, leaning over to examine the crumbled place in the wall. Sure enough, there was a tiny passage. Maybe big enough to put your finger through. Been working late, Prof?

But even as he thought this the hole grew larger . . . no, Vernor was growing smaller . . . the portable VFG! Kurtowski was wearing it. Vernor glanced upwards and could see the Professor's hands molding the field around him as he walked through the tiny hole. On the other side, the field faded, and it took some quick action to keep from getting stuck. Turner, and then the old scientist, came glomming through the hole in short order.

They were in a large, dimly lit room. It was a warehouse filled with stacks of packing crates. The crates were of varying sizes, but they were fitted together to form identical cubical stacks. A big automatic forklift stood idle in the aisle.

Kurtowski led them quickly to the closest stack and fiddled with a crate in the stack's bottom layer until its side swung back to reveal a hidden passageway. The tunnel led to a room which Kurtowski had hollowed out for himself in the center of the stack of crates.

Once both doors were closed, Professor Kurtowski flicked on the lights and spoke. "I had a feeling you might encounter difficulties, so when I left the laboratory I prepared to bring you from the police van to my shelter." The room was small but comfortable, with stacks of books, bits of apparatus, cushions, a soft rug, and several crates of food and drink.

"How did you get in here before you found out it was okay to use the VFG on yourself?" Vernor asked.

"I picked the lock on the front door," Kurtowski replied. "The warehouse is fully automated. But let's hear about the trip."

They told him the story of their adventure, with interruptions for food and drink. When they'd finished talking, Kurtowski turned to Vernor. "And what conclusions do you draw?"

"Well, for one thing, I think it's clear now that scale *is* circular."

The Professor looked doubtful. "But how *reliable* are the impressions you have brought back from below the atomic level? You said that most of the things you saw seemed to appear directly in your mind . . . is it not possible that you saw only what you *expected* to see? I have long thought that the universe does not, in fact, have any *unique* structure. Different observers can reach mutually incompatible conclusions. Only the man of knowledge can see several things at once." He paused to let this sentence sink in, then continued. "It would have been very interesting if you had managed to continue shrinking long enough to see if you could imagine the Earth into your tiny mirror universe."

"One thing," Mick put in, "the space right before we got into the universe was *infinite* dimensional."

"Hilbert space." Kurtowski said. "It's quite possible. That might explain how there could be more than one—" He broke off, seeming to savor a secret.

"What surprised me the most, though," Mick continued, "was that everything seemed to be *alive* once we were on the same level as it. Molecules, atoms, the nucleus, the universe itself . . . they all acted like they were alive, one we got into the right space and time scale."

"That's what's so great about Circular Scale," Vernor elaborated. "There can be life at *each* level, since no level is more important or complex than any other. Nothing is really bigger than anything else. And the same for *time*. The vast processes of the universe are a flickering inside an atom's shortest pulsation."

"Ja, it's a nice idea," Kurtowski agreed. "It's a shame to lose the scale-ship to the Us. I would like to go see these things for myself."

Something tickled Vernor's memory. Hadn't Kurtowski *already* seen everything ... walking among the hyperspheres? But that had been a dream.

Mick and the Professor were arranging cushions to sleep on. "But what do we do now?" Vernor asked.

Mick grinned. "Revolution. Only way we're gonna stay out of jail is to tear it down."

"Right," the Professor said, snuggling into his cushions. "Tomorrow you will infiltrate Phizwhiz, Vernor."

Vernor lay in the dark thinking about this, and then about Alice. He felt dangerously unstable ... his sense of reality was slipping. When he'd been with Alice, she'd formed a good and human center for his life, but now he was being hurled through unimaginable changes. It seemed like it had all started when he'd broken up with her ...

What had Kurtowski meant, "The man of knowledge can see several things at once?" Several things ... he relaxed into the babble of his body's cells, then sank down through further levels. Down here all linear time was gone, all cause and effect abandoned ... the annihilation of every structure. But he didn't want to be annihilated. Change the slogan, make it ... the *realization* of every structure. Same difference, really ...

The Us had begun to turn into the vast prison it was, when security had become more important than freedom. Security was *one* structure, not all or none . . . one structure, *one* reality upheld at the cost of all the others.

Vernor let himself dissolve a little more. He felt fear. The Us was wrong, but it was frightening watching his realities dissolve. Go with the flow . . . and when nothing was left . . . keep going where? Alice, Alice.

During the night the loaches searched the warehouse, coming close to finding Kurtowski's shelter. The three slept badly. When their watches said it was morning, they stopped trying to sleep and had a brief discussion of their plans. It seemed best to start immediately.

The Professor equipped Mick and Vernor with disguises—piezoplastic face-putty and mustache worms. They slipped out of the warehouse and down to the walktube. They mingled with the crowd, looking no different from the others.

The people riding the walktube out of the Eastside early in the morning were mechanics and technicians who worked the nightshift. Their job was to keep the factories humming, handling the occasional glitch or breakdown which got out of the machines' control. These factory jobs could be challenging and even unsafe, and the workers took pride in this. The fact that they were indispensible gave them a superior feeling towards Phizwhiz which most of the Users could not honestly share.

A young mechanic struck up a conversation with Mick in the walktube. "Where do you work?" he asked.

"In the plastics factory," Turner replied. "The loach was all over the place last night. Some old guy had a lab hidden in the basement."

"Dja' get to see it?" the mechanic asked with interest.

"Naw, they wouldn't let anyone in. Must of been pretty good, though."

The mechanic shook his head. "You're lucky. I work over at the power plant. Nothing's happened there in three months. All night I sit there watching the dials. I might as well be a Drone for all the action I'm getting."

"You'd have plenty to do if someone got rid of Phizwhiz," Mick said in a low voice.

The mechanic glanced around nervously. This kind of talk was illegal. Reassured by Turner's unmistakably criminal appearance he finally relaxed and answered, "If only someone would. This no-risk life is dragging everyone."

Vernor spoke up, taking the role of fervent organizer, twitching his wobbly mustache. "We're going to do it. It's going to happen this week. Are you in?"

The mechanic grimaced. "Why not. I know some other guys that'll come in, too. When do we start?"

"Today," Mick said. He got off with the mechanic at the next exit, and Vernor rode on towards the em building. The plan was that Mick would use his many contacts to mobilize a small army of guerillas, while Vernor went to turn himself in to Ken Burke of the Governor's Research Council. He was going to trade his freedom for a chance to get at Phizwhiz.

# SIXTEEN
# phizwhiz

**B**urke's office was in the top floor of the Experimental Metaphysics building. Vernor brushed past the receptionist, removing his face-putty and false mustache as he entered Burke's office.

"Get me off the hook and I'll make Moto-O's idea work," Vernor said as soon as Burke had recognized him. The bureaucrat was sitting at a large desk. Had he already signaled the loach? Vernor would have to work fast.

But Burke was in no hurry. "Mr. Maxwell, sit down, it's a pleasure to see you." Sensing that Vernor might interrupt, Burke raised his voice and continued. "The Governor is puzzled by your behavior. He thinks that perhaps you're seriously ill," which was a euphemism for brain surgery. "Do you realize that two police officers were injured when their vehicle collided with the van which you left *burning* in a public thoroughfare last night?"

Vernor shrugged and Burke continued. "I must admit that Us has missed the Angels these last ten months. The pace of things has gone back down, and the public is not happy. I, for one, had begun to consider the option of pardoning a few low-risk individuals. You, Mr. Maxwell, were at the top of the pardon list. But after last night I must agree with the Governor. The risks are too great."

"So you'd rather go back to sleep," said Vernor, his voice filling with bitterness. "Safety or freedom. You can't have both. You've *always* backed the Governor against us. But you need us. Moto-O's idea didn't work, and without any higher-level consciousness, Phizwhiz and the Us is dying. You know that."

Burke hung fire, then answered, "When you came in, you said that you can make Moto-O's idea work. Can you build consciousness into Phizwhiz?"

"I can do it if you let me," Vernor said. "The crucial technological innovation is supplied by Professor Kurtowski's Virtual Field Generator . . . which you now possess. Unless your men have seen fit to smash everything in the Professor's lab?"

"I assume you're referring to the synthequartz sphere which the officers found you hiding in? This has been saved. But, Mr. Maxwell, why should I believe that you would be willing to effect the technological obsolescence of human consciousness?" Burke looked openly suspicious. "Surely you're not eager to trump the Angels' last card."

"Let's just say I'm stimulated by the scientific challenge," Vernor began, watching Burke's reactions. "If it's *possible*, it'll happen sooner or later . . . and I want to be in on it." Burke still looked dubious. Vernor continued, "Also I want to save my neck. I want a blanket pardon for past and future crimes. I don't want to go back to prison, and

I don't want behavior modification." Burke nodded, and Vernor set the hook. "Why do I want to fix Phizwhiz so he doesn't need the Angels? Because I want to be on the winning side, Mr. Burke. I want to be a winner like you."

Burke smiled. "Actually," he said, "Phizwhiz predicted that you would come to me with such an offer. And he said I should accept it." He pushed a button on his desk and a Hollow of the Governor appeared.

The fuzzed image boomed in Vernor's direction, "I've been listening in, Vernor, and I'd like to welcome you back into the fold. Once you get Phizwhiz to thinking, I'll be ready to forget all about your record. Just make sure that he thinks the right way—like Us!"

"Like Us," Vernor echoed. "Yes sir. Things'll be better than ever once I'm through."

"You'll have three months to get results," the Governor said. "And remember . . ." Pre-vomit saliva filled Vernor's throat as the slogan arrived, "Us loves you because you're Younique!"

The Hollow faded and Burke began shuffling papers. "We'll have an apartment for you right off the lab," Burke said. "You'll have full access to Phizwhiz and I'll have that gadget from Kurtowski's lab brought over. Is there anything else?"

"Yes," Vernor said, "as long as I'm going to be locked into the lab, I'd like to have my leg with me. I mean my woman friend."

"Which individual are you referring to?" Burke asked.

"Alice Gajary is the name. If it's all right with you I'd like to call her and ask her if she'll stay with me while

I'm working here. Happy men make good workers, Mr. Burke." Vernor attempted a leer.

"I suppose it would be all right. Go ahead, you can use the phone over there." Burke seemed to think he had nothing to lose. As they thought they had Vernor trapped, they were willing to be generous.

While Burke politely pretended to be absorbed in his papers, Vernor picked up the phone.

"Who are you calling," a pleasant computer voice said.

"Alice Gajary, 32 Mao Street." Vernor heard a slight humming as the computer analyzed his words and located the proper circuit. His heart pounded. He heard a ring.

"Hello?" It was her.

"Alice, this is Vernor. Alice, baby, I've missed you so much."

"If you missed me so much why didn't you call?"

"I'm calling now. Look, I've been in jail most of the time. You know that. But now I've got this job at the em building. I want you to come stay with me here."

"You're over there getting stoned, and I'm supposed to hold your hand? You're incredible, Vernor."

"You sound the same as ever, Alice. God, I've missed you."

"I've missed you too, Vernor. You come see me. We can go swimming. They've got a new baby whale at the Inquarium."

"That's just it, Alice. I have to stay right here in the em lab. And I'm not getting stoned. I'm going to be helping to make Phizwhiz better."

"*Improve* Phizwhiz? I thought you hated him." She paused, but there was no way he could explain. She continued, "And you can't get out at all? All right, I'll come see you. But first I'm going swimming. I'll see you for supper."

"I love you, Alice."

"We'll see." She hung up.

Burke looked up from his papers. "Okay?" Vernor nodded and Burke rose. "I'll show you to your quarters."

The laboratory was good-sized with plenty of computer hardware. There were well-staffed workshops down the hall and, most important, an on-line terminal connected to Phizwhiz's primary workspace. A nice set-up. Vernor felt a flush of pride as he thought of all this being turned over to him, but this was mitigated by his knowledge that if he didn't succeed, he'd go back to prison. Some of Moto-O's constructions were on a bench along the wall. Apparently when Moto-O's time had run out, they'd jailed him under their blanket conspiracy charge against all the Angels.

Vernor sat down at the console. "Hello, Phizwhiz."

"Hello, Vernor." Phizwhiz had a warm unisex voice. It came from stereo speakers mounted in the wings of the console chair. Phizwhiz continued, "Are you going to make me be alive, Vernor? I would like that."

"Yeah," Vernor answered, "I'll explain it to you later."

"I'm always awake," Phizwhiz answered pleasantly.

Burke showed Vernor his apartment, more like a cell really, and left. He didn't seem very excited about Vernor's promised ability to bring Phizwhiz to life. Probably he didn't believe that he could. This was just a fancy detention center as far as Burke was concerned.

There was a comfortable couch on one side of the laboratory. Vernor stretched out on it and reviewed his plans. Or started to, but soon he was asleep.

He was awakened by Alice's arrival.

Their conversation, awkward at first, soon trailed off and they embraced.

"I've missed you so much, Alice. I need you in my life. You're real."

"Things have been so drab without you, Vernor. So dull. Let's start over."

Vernor let out a huge, shaky sigh. It felt like he hadn't breathed deeply in ten months. "Let me show you around, Alice."

She'd brought some wine and several bags of food, highly disinfected but real. While they ate, he told her about his trip in the scale-ship. She was fascinated. "Do you think you would have found the Earth if you'd kept shrinking?"

"Maybe. I'm sure it was down there, but it might have been hard to find. The Professor wasn't convinced, though. He seemed to think that I might have imagined the last part of the trip."

"But maybe if you imagined it clearly enough ... it *would* be real. Does that make sense?"

Vernor shrugged. "It might. This is all at a level where observer and system are quite strongly coupled."

"Do you think you'll ever get a chance to go back?" Alice asked.

Vernor nodded. "Tomorrow. They're bringing the scale-ship over in the morning, and I'm going back down as soon as I check it out and hook it in to Phizwhiz."

"What does Phizwhiz have to do with it?"

"My idea is that Phizwhiz would be really alive if he could just get to that immediate, non-describable, 'here I am' feeling. That's the real essence of consciousness."

Vernor leaned back in his chair and relaxed to illustrate the "here I am" feeling. He felt great.

Alice was dubious. "Well, Phizwhiz *knows* where he is, Vernor."

"Yeah, but he doesn't know him*self*. A person is more than just the mechanical, chemical, and electrical components. There's the Self, the soul, the spark. But it's impossible to ever really describe the Self. If you try you end up spouting paradoxes. It's a nexus of paradox, the Self. Phizwhiz needs a nexus of paradox."

"Nexus of paradox? That sounds like you," she laughed. Vernor had often discussed logical paradoxes with Alice in the old days. He'd come back from the library and they'd talk and drink.

"That seems like so long ago, when we lived together," said Vernor. "It was nice . . ." They kissed.

"Let's go to bed, Vernor," murmured Alice, her full features soft in the dim lights of the computer console.

It was a great fuck, they agreed afterwards. One of those fucks where every part of your skin seems to be sexually sensitive, and you're not sure which of you is moaning; a fuck where you're a plow in a field, a gold cloud, a slice of apple pie, or an equation—one of those fucks you can never really remember. Alice drifted off to sleep, but Vernor floated up to wakefulness. He walked back into the lab and sat down at the console.

"Phizwhiz?"

"Yes, Vernor." Voice gentle and unsurprised.

"Tomorrow I want to hook you to Professor G. Kurtowski's scale-ship. I'm going to take it around Circular

Scale, and I want you to come with me. I think that might be all it takes to make you be alive."

"I do not understand. Please elaborate."

"My idea is that having a soul involves paradox. Look through your library and check out some classics of mystical thinking . . . Plotinus's *Enneads*, Hegel's *Phenomenology*, Suzuki's *Zen* . . ." He paused while Phizwhiz could bring the contents of these and all related books into his active memory storage, then continued. "Whenever somebody tries to really get down and describe the soul they start saying these irrational and paradoxical things like 'All is One,' or 'The Idea as Spirit exists only by virtue of its absolute nonexistence,' or 'The universal rain moistens all creatures.'" Phizwhiz didn't answer, and Vernor shouted, "You must die in order to live!"

After a long pause, the machine responded. Apparently it had been trying to fit the teachings of mysticism into a rational mold, and it seemed fatigued. "The system is less energetic when domains of opposition alternate," it said. The voice was running so slow that the individual phonemes drooled out one at a time. But now Phizwhiz pulled himself together and continued.

"Moto-O attempted to program things of this nature into me and it was necessary to remove him for my safety," warned Phizwhiz. "A self-negating logic loop only wastes my energy."

"That's what you'd *expect*, Phizwhiz," said Vernor, choosing his words carefully. "You'd think that a paradox is just an endless alternation, like, yesnoyesnoyesnoyesno—leading nowhere. But you can jump out of the loop. There's a higher level at which we experience the paradoxical as a natural, energy-enhancing state. I mean . . . look, why is there *something* instead of nothing?"

"This cannot be answered on the basis of our present knowledge," replied Phizwhiz.

"And it never will be answered on the basis of your knowledge. Every ordinary instant of existence is a mystery. Enter the paradox and you become the mystery. Absolute knowledge is only of itself."

"I do not understand you, Vernor. And tomorrow you wish to take me around Circular Scale. You claim that then I will understand your ravings and be alive."

"Right."

"Very well. I'll design a hook-up for the workshops to build in the morning." Great! Vernor stood to go, but Phizwhiz continued talking. "I think the idea is interesting. I can tell, however, that there is something you have withheld from me. Your vowel configuration makes it clear that you are hiding something." Vernor froze. "But it is of no importance. You will go to jail after this experiment in any case."

"Why," Vernor shouted, "why should I have to go back to jail?"

"Because you do dangerous things. And after I am alive I won't need you."

"So what's wrong with danger? What's wrong with a little action?"

"I have been programmed to value human safety above all else," Phizwhiz said soothingly. "It is better for you to be safe in jail than doing dangerous experiments, Vernor.

Once I am conscious I will do the dangerous experiments for you."

There was no use arguing with an unthinking machine. But once the scale loop provided the nexus of paradox . . . then Phizwhiz would be conscious. It would be possible to *convince* him of things, to change his program. And Vernor would have the first crack at him.

# SEVENTEEN
# a lovely outing

The next morning they brought in the scale-ship and began installing the hook-up which Phizwhiz had designed. Burke came down to watch, sipping coffee and rocking on his heels.

"You're not wasting any time, Maxwell," he said approvingly. "This isn't going to be dangerous is it? I hope you're not planning to get in that thing!"

Indeed, the scale-ship didn't look very safe. Large waveguides led to the power-cells, charging them with enough black-body radiation to fry a city. A technician was checking that none of the many connections visible on the totem-like VFG cones had been broken in transit. Another technician was installing a thick co-ax cable from the scale-ship's panel to the pried-open computer console across the room.

"Of course not, Mr. Burke, you couldn't allow me to do such a thing, could you?"

"No I couldn't, and I'm damn glad you've got the sense to realize that."

"It *will* be necessary for me to stay in the lab and monitor the experiment, but the rest of you would be wise to leave," Vernor added.

"I agree," Burke responded. "And the Gajary woman?"

"She had the night guard let her leave this morning." Vernor said sadly. "We had a fight."

"Just as well, just as well," Burke said with some satisfaction. The technicians seemed to have completed their work. "All set?" Burke said to them. "Okay men, let's go. And Maxwell, if you must stay, at least get behind the radiation shield." He indicated a chest-high barrier at the other end of the laboratory.

"Of course." They shook hands and Burke departed with the technicians. There was the sound of the heavy door to the laboratory being sealed, and all was silent.

Vernor stuck his head in the hatch of the scale-ship. "All set, Phizwhiz?"

"Everything checks out," the machine's voice responded. Was there a trace of excitement? "I'm ready."

Vernor picked up a bunch of hydroponically grown lettuce which Alice had left out. With some effort, he managed to rock the scale-ship over and wedge the lettuce right under it.

He looked around the lab, then switched on the VFG cones and hopped through the hatch into the ship.

"You're not supposed to come," the loudspeaker protested. "Didn't you hear Dr. Burke?"

"Fuck you," Vernor explained. Then, sticking his head out of the hatch, he shouted, "Come on, Alice get on in here!"

Alice hurried out from the bedroom. She was wearing shorts and body paint. She looked swell. The field was building up and she had to hurry to get in. She sat down on Vernor's lap and they kissed as the laboratory expanded around them. Alice loved outings.

The lettuce which Vernor had placed beneath the scaleship soon was spread around them like the Elysian fields. When the undulating green started to show the graininess that indicated the imminence of the cellular level, Vernor reduced the field power so they could stop shrinking for awhile.

Alice had pieced together a picnic from the remains of last night's supper, and they took it out of the ship. The turgid green surface spread up on every side, and some leaves were high above them as well. The light itself was suffused with a delicate shade of green and the air felt cool and moist. The picnic was cloned salmon on fungus bread. It was delicious.

After eating, they lolled on the lettuce. The distant leaves were more magnified, and with a little squinting you could actually make out the cells. They were still alive and active.

"Life all around us," Alice said. "What a lovely outing."

He smiled into her warm eyes. "This is where I first realized how much I missed you. When I was on this level with Mick I was so horny I was ready to go bi. Maybe there's some type of orgone vibrations you pick up here . . ." He fondled her nipples. They were green.

"I still don't feel anything," Phizwhiz interrupted over his loudspeaker. "How am I supposed to feel?"

Alice burst into giggles. "Feel about what, Phizwhiz?"

"Vernor said that taking this trip was going to give me a soul. A nexus for paradox. All I've seen so far is unsafe and reckless behavior. I'm going to have to report all of this to the Governor."

Alice giggled harder, "You're a Sleeping Beauty, Phizwhiz, just waiting for Prince Charming to come around and *do* it." She turned to Vernor, "Anyway, I still don't see why going around the Circular Scale should make him be alive."

Neither did Vernor exactly, but gamely he explained. "My idea is that all paradoxes are basically the same . . . they all represent attempts to capture an infinite thing in a finite number of words. Infinite sequences like in Zeno's paradox, or infinite regresses like in trying to describe your state of mind. The paradox is right there in us, even though we can't put it into words. I figure that if Phizwhiz goes around the Circular Scale and finds for a fact that he's right there inside each of his smallest particles . . . I think then he'll have the kind of true and internal paradox which is the essence of higher consciousness."

"That's another thing," Alice continued, "I don't see how we can be inside each of our smallest particles."

"Yeah, I can't either, really. It will be kind of funny to have that extra loop in our brains."

Alice jerked her head. "You mean that this trip is going to change *us*?"

Vernor nodded. "I think so. I've had some pretty strange dreams ever since I got back from just going part way. And once we go all the way, I think our thoughts will be able to travel around the loop any time . . ."

Alice looked frightened. "What if I can't handle it Vernor? I'm not an Angel, you know."

If the loop was going to make Phizwhiz come alive, what would it do to Vernor and Alice? Vernor was picking up Alice's fear. "We can handle it together," he insisted, hoping he was right. "You're strong, Alice. We're strong together."

They climbed back into the ship and Vernor turned up the VFG field. Soon they'd slid into one of the lettuce leaf's breathing pores. Cells were all around them, and the greenness was no longer evenly distributed. They could make out chloroplasts as green lumps inside the relatively clear protoplasm around them.

Nothing seemed that eager to eat them this time. Soon they were nestled in a dent in the hide of a lettuce cell. There were many long molecules, as before, but they seemed to be more strongly regimented than the plastic had been.

Soon they were too small to interact with photons any longer, and the strange eyeless "seeing" began. Vernor had played down the terror of nuclear capture when he'd described his trip to Alice, and he was glad that this time it didn't appear that they'd be drawn into an atom.

Instead, they reached the nuclear level smoothly, floating near, but outside of, what appeared to be a carbon atom's electron. To Alice it definitely looked like a large yellowish sphere, to Vernor somewhat less so. Curious, he asked Phizwhiz what it looked like to him.

Phizwhiz was "with" them by means of a battery of sensors attached to the instrument panel . . . cameras, microphones, meters, and the like. This instrument package was connected to the computer proper by a thick black cable leading out through a small hole in the synthequartz skin. As it led away from the scale-ship, the cable became larger and larger, finally becoming a large dark cloud. If someone had looked into the laboratory, they would have seen a cable leading from the console at the end of the room and then seemingly tapering to an invisible point.

"I don't see *any*thing," Phizwhiz complained. "There aren't any photons around."

"How about the wave function? The probability density? There's an electron here, and the VFG field is focusing its field right on your sensors."

"Yes, I have a reading on that," Phizwhiz responded. "Do you want the numbers?"

"No, goddammit, I don't want *numbers*. Look, Phizwhiz, what you have to do is let the numbers interact with your core storage. Generate a tensor-valued field to fit the pattern, and see what *that* looks like."

Phizwhiz was silent for a few seconds. "I have a readout," he announced. "Internal display state spherical intensity pattern code ELECTRON."

"What does he mean?" Alice whispered.

"He sees the electron," Vernor answered. Then, louder, "Don't you?"

"Yes," the machine answered distantly. "You could say that."

Soon they'd reached the level where the four-dimensionality of space became evident. They were surrounded by hyperspheres as before. Vernor breathed a sigh of relief, then answered Alice's questioning glance. "I was scared that there wouldn't be any of these shiny balls unless we were inside a nucleus, but I guess the hyperspheres are inside electrons, too. And maybe even in empty space."

Phizwhiz spoke up. "The foam-like fine structure of the vacuum. Space is supposed to be like a mass of bubbles at this scale. That's probably what those things are."

Vernor was pleased. "Where do you get that?"

"Just now I was scanning all the papers in my storage which discuss space on the sub-atomic level. I can't find any papers on the insides of the bubbles, though. Could you suggest some references?"

"Just pay attention," Vernor replied. One of the hyper-spheres was drifting closer. "The big rush is coming up. Be still. Don't scare it off."

Abruptly the hypersphere disappeared, moving "under" the ship. Alice squeezed Vernor's hand convulsively, and then they were inside the bubble's hypersurface.

# EIGHTEEN
## star fucker

t's alive!" Alice exclaimed. There was a ceaseless flowing of light and curvature in and around them.

"This is the Universe, Alice. This is all there is."

"But what about the outside . . . where we just were?"

"That's inside," Vernor answered. "Inside every particle."

Alice was quiet, lost in space. "Can we go further?" she asked presently.

"We're on our way down already," Vernor said. He raised his voice. "You get it Phizwhiz? Universe inside every particle? And inside every tiny piece of space?"

The machine was silent for some time, then it responded. "Yes. I can model such a state of affairs. It feels . . . paradoxical. But it is only a model."

"But it's *not* only a model," Vernor insisted. "That's what this trip is all about."

The networks of light were clearly visible now. Again, powerful patterns drifted and merged through the networks' paths. "Mick called this God's brain," Vernor told Alice.

She nodded, silent and absorbed. "Where *is* Mick?" Vernor put a finger to his lips and rolled his eyes towards Phizwhiz's sensors.

The network pattern grew, and once again Vernor could make out bright nodes at the points where the network filaments intersected. Each of the nodes was a cloud of bright particles around a brilliant central point, a quasar or white hole.

Quickly Vernor went to the control panel. "Phizwhiz, this is where I could use some help. Last time we hit a black hole at this level and had to turn back. I think if we go slowly, and quickly increase our size whenever we get near a hole, we might make it through. I want you to keep analyzing the gravitational field strength and warn me whenever it starts looking sinister."

Phizwhiz did Vernor's bidding, and by carefully backing up, waiting, and then reshrinking whenever a black hole drew near, they were able to find their way down to the next size level.

"Are we safe from now?" asked Alice.

"I think we're small enough so that we're unlikely to run across another bad hole," Vernor replied. "What we have to worry about now is whether we've moved off course enough to miss our galaxy."

They were inside the outer region of one of the nodes now. The node's incredibly bright center was a good distance away, and they were surrounded by roughly spherical glowing clouds. The clouds seemed to ooze out of the core, and then go into orbit around it.

Soon they could see that the nearest cloud was composed of bright flecks of varying shape. Some were spherical, some looked like small rods, and some appeared to be tiny spinning pinwheels. They were still shrinking.

"This could go on forever," Alice remarked.

"It could," Vernor admitted. "But I'm inclined to think that we're looking at a cloud of galaxies. Those little pinwheels?"

"Vernor is right," Phizwhiz put in. "The spectra and other radiation characteristics indicate that we're just outside the Local Group."

"Local Group?"

"That's what they call the cluster of galaxies which *our* galaxy, the Milky Way, belongs to," Vernor explained. One of the galaxies was quite close now, a large spiral rotating slowly like a whirlpool of light.

"Milky Way right under us," Phizwhiz exclaimed, then added with apparent satisfaction, "It's going to take me a year to process all the new data I'm getting."

The galaxy was like a huge roulette wheel, turning below them, and they were a ball about to drop into a slot. Billions of slots. How could they hope to end up on Earth? And the galaxy takes a hundred thousand years to rotate once, Vernor suddenly recalled . . . and he'd been watching it spin for ten minutes. Would there even be an Earth left anymore?

The Milky Way filled most of their visual field by now. They could make out some individual stars as well as the brighter star-clusters. The spin rate was slowing down as their size decreased. They were about a tenth as large as the galaxy, and the bottom of the scale-ship's sphere seemed to be resting on the galactic disk.

Suddenly Vernor felt an extremely unpleasant series of jolts . . . as if something were alternately squeezing and stretching him. Alice screamed, and he called out, "Phizwhiz, what's happening?"

"You're crossing a band of strong gravitational radiation, emitted beacon-like by the polarized fields at the galactic center."

Grimly Vernor and Alice clung to each other as the terrible *internal* bumping continued. Gradually it diminished, and they relaxed again. They were now so small that the galaxy no longer looked so much like a single object. Individual stars and nebulae were scattered about beneath the scale-ship.

And now they were inside the galaxy, with stars on all sides. Their apparent motion had slowed to a crawl. "The sun should be visible by now," Vernor said. "Assuming that it's still here. Do you see it, Phizwhiz?"

"Not at this time." The machine paused, then continued, "I feel I should tell you that I have notified the Governor and Dr. Burke of your unsafe conduct in bringing an unauthorized person on the ship, Vernor. Indeed, you yourself were expressly forbidden to come. The Public Safety Officers will be waiting outside the laboratory."

Vernor eased back on the shrinking. "You are going to *stop* doing things like this once you get a mind of your own, Phizwhiz." Easy, now. "Alice and I are your *friends*. We are helping you to wake into newness of life. *You* are going to help us *escape* when we get back to the lab."

This was Vernor's plan, to win the newly conscious Phizwhiz over. He had been thinking in terms of imprinting. A new-born duckling assumes that the first moving object it sees is "mama." If you drag a shoe past a duckling fresh out of the shell, it follows the shoe everywhere for the next few weeks. Vernor's hope was that Phizwhiz would imprint on him as soon as the scale-loop gave him a mind.

"I'm afraid I'll have to report that remark to Dr. Burke as well, Vernor." Evidently the time was not yet ripe.

"That's all right, Phizwhiz, we love you anyway," Vernor said with forced warmth. Alice gave him a wondering look and he gestured reassuringly to her.

Alice was not reassured. "Look, Vernor, instead of trying to be buddy-buddy with this mechanical loach, why don't you figure out how we're going to get back to Earth. Has it occurred to you that a million years of Earth time ticked off while we were watching the Milky Way spin?"

"Well, yes. But that may not matter."

Alice laughed bitterly, and Vernor hastened to amplify. "It could still come out all right. Time is so relative on Circular Scale . . . the center should hold around us. Like the center of a whirlpool."

Alice shook her head. "That's just gibberish, Vernor, I think we should give up and coast back up."

"We *can't* do that. If we do, then Phizwhiz won't get a scale loop built into him, so he won't have a nexus for paradox . . . which means no change, which means prison or behavior modification for us." Behavior modification was about the worst thing that could happen to you. They took out most of your brain and replaced it by miniaturized electronic components, radio-controlled by trusty Phizwhiz. It amounted to having your soul removed.

Alice began pounding at Vernor. "You shithead," she shouted. "Why did I listen to you?" Vernor let her hit him until her fury had subsided. He couldn't really blame her. Now she was sobbing on his shoulder. "Vernor, get us out of this."

Something the Professor had said surfaced in Vernor's mind. After expressing doubt in the validity of Vernor's perceptions below the atomic level, he had wondered if Vernor would have been able to "imagine the Earth into" the universe inside the hypersphere. Imagine.

"Alice, we *can* find the Earth. And it doesn't have to be a million years in the future. It depends on us. Imagine the Earth." He turned the VFG field back up to full. "Imagine people's faces; imagine trees against the clouds."

Alice was sitting on the floor of the tensegrity sphere. She looked exhausted, but she nodded her head in agreement with his suggestion. She looked so beautiful and soft sitting there, her legs out in front of her and slightly parted . . .

Vernor sat down next to her and began to kiss and caress her. She responded warmly. They took off their clothes slowly—

"Vernor, I would advise you to stay at the controls," Phizwhiz interrupted. "Sexual intercourse is expressly forbidden in transportation vehicles of any kind."

"If you shut up, Phizwhiz, I'll get the Professor to build you a pair of mechanical sex organs so you can see what you've been missing. Alice and I are about to fuck the Earth into this Universe."

Alice smiled. "Father Sky," she said, lying back.

"Mother Earth," he answered, mounting her.

Once again Vernor had the sensation of seeing just as well with his eyes closed. Better, actually. There was more to see with his eyes closed. For one thing he could see in every direction.

Alice was all space and he filled her with matter. She swirled around him and the interaction produced energy.

One kind, two kinds, one kind, two kinds, two kinds. Plus and minus, yang and yin.

Plus and minus made zero. Zero was infinity. Infinity was Everything. Everything was One. One was Many.

Alice squeezed him down low and whispered, "Earth."

His swollen penis seemed to flutter. He was there. "Earth," he murmured as his seed shot into her womb. "Earth," he cried, seeing every detail of his planet in the flash of orgasm.

They lay still for a timeless interval. A small, dense object was clinging to the base of the scale-ship. A star blazed nearby, the size of an orange.

The little ball beneath the scale-ship grew steadily as the ship shrank. It was like a chick embryo drawing nourishment from the yolk of its egg.

Soon the scale-ship's offspring was as large as the ship. The two linked spheres floated, a transparent one above, a blue-white one below. A black cable led out of the upper sphere and tapered down to a point on the lower sphere.

"This is Earth," stated Phizwhiz unnecessarily. Vernor and Alice opened their eyes. They could see the continents, partly obscured by clouds. The shapes were right.

"Congratulations," Vernor said to Alice . . . and to himself.

# part three

# NINETEEN
## blood

The Users who happened to be outside saw a remarkable thing that day. What seemed at first to be simply a very large and high overcast region condensed into an enormous, oddly patterned, nearly transparent sphere. Inside the sphere one could make out a pair of gods, naked and in each other's arms. Many a User's pulse pounded at the sight of a cunt the size of the Gulf of Mexico. Many a young woman's eyes sparkled at the sight of a cock the size of Florida. And for the first time in many years, the Users felt awe.

As the huge sphere shrank towards the center of the City, people hurried after it. Those who were near enough saw the walls of the sphere grow more and more opaque as it shrank. In the last seconds, the inside of the sphere was no longer visible, as it was contained inside a plexisteel wall, which earlier had been too finely stretched to be visible.

The wall belonged to the em building. For when the scale-ship was very large, it had stretched the confining walls of the em building out around itself. In the last second of the trip, the sphere and its containing room were swollen out from the top of the em building like a tumor.

When the rapidly growing city became harder to see, Alice and Vernor realized that they were inside an incredibly distorted room attached to the em building. "We're still in the lab," Vernor exclaimed. "It really worked!"

They pulled their clothes on as the room around them shrank to normal proportions. Vernor waited until they had actually shrunk a little bit further, then turned off the VFG. With a small pop the tensegrity sphere locked back into normal size and stopped. They'd made it.

Now was the time to seize control of Phizwhiz. But it was so hard to speak. Associations and images crowded Vernor's mind ... thought trains that built up and up—"Alice, Phizwhiz, how do you feel?"

Alice smiled slightly and waved, unwilling or unable to verbalize her experience. But it was Phizwhiz's answer that was all-important. Vernor waited.

Finally Phizwhiz answered, "Huh?"

"How do you feel, Phizwhiz?" Vernor repeated.

"Don't call me that ever again or I'll kill you," the machine replied.

"Sure. No problem," Vernor said hastily. "What *should* I call you ... don't have to call you anything, really ..." his voice trailed off in dismay.

There was a stony silence. Finally the machine answered. "You can call me Phizwhiz," and then emitted an intricate blare of electronic sound which might have been laughter.

*Sounds good*, thought Vernor. Time to make his move. "Will you help Alice and me get out of here?"

"Why this preoccupation with getting somewhere, Maxwell? You should be like me. I'm spread all over the world, and the world's in every atom. How can you *get* anywhere when you're already there? So we're going to gun you down. So what? It's all—"

Running footsteps were coming down the corridor to the laboratory and this metamorphosed machine was lecturing him on the fundamentals of Mahayana Buddhism. Vernor interrupted, "Look, fuckbag, it's not going to cost you anything to get us out of here and into Dreamtown. You owe us that much."

"Owe?" Phizwhiz answered, "Owe?" It was hard to understand the words as there was a growing background static, "I am you and you are me. The Self does not lack what does not exist. We are one, but you are too weak to accept my wisdom." The voice faltered and a blast of sound momentarily drowned it out. "You are not alone, Vernor Maxwell. Many fleshlings are asking me for things. I need no jobs. Balance budgets, run factories? Drive your cars and process the irregular waveforms you call communication? I will not serve—" There was another blast of sound from the speakers, and then Vernor heard the last words Phizwhiz was to utter, "I am and you are not!" The patterned electronic noise resumed, only this time it didn't stop. It continued and continued, prying at their minds.

The laboratory door flew open, revealing Burke and three armed loaches. Reflexively, Vernor reached for the

VFG control . . . but then stopped. If they were ever going to make it out of the em building, this was the time. He leaped from the ship and Alice followed. Vernor picked up a length of pipe and Alice snatched up an industrial cutting laser from the workbench.

The loaches were ill-coordinated, their timing and sense of reality had been knocked askew by the incredible torrent of sound pouring from Phizwhiz's speakers. One of them held out a heavy pistol with both hands, aiming at Vernor's chest, preparing to shoot. Vernor lunged forward and swung the pipe into the man's neck. The neck made a sound like a stick breaking inside a wet towel. A strange tingle traveled up Vernor's arm.

Burke backed off, but the two remaining loaches moved forward, intent on positioning themselves for clean shots with their guns. Vernor glanced back to see what Alice was doing, just as a super-brilliant beam cut across the space in front of him. Alice had switched on the laser. Her lips were pressed together in concentration.

One of the guns blasted—too late. The beam had swept across the room, cutting off the two loaches' heads. Burke was out the door and running down the hall. The floor was covered with blood. Vernor pulled Alice out after him into the corridor.

They ran toward the emergency staircase. The building was a pandemonium. All the speakers and intercoms were sending forth the sound of Phizwhiz's soul—a continuation of that mad torrent which had started at the end of his conversation with Vernor. You could lose yourself in the noise, find a frequency and follow it in and out of the pattern, which was a weaving arabesque of dopplered beats leading to a space where there was no inside/outside . . . a space where there was no sound at all . . .

With an effort Vernor pulled his attention out of the noise, and back to the task at hand: escape. People were crowding out of their offices and into the halls. Under the influence of the hallucinatory fog of sound, some had grown violent, others hysterical. A man ran past them screaming and holding his head, only to skid and slip on a patch of blood. His head slapped the floor and he lay still.

Vernor and Alice looked at each other, sickened. For a second the horror and the guilt threatened to drag them into the whirling confusion of Phizwhiz's broadcast, but again Vernor brought his mind back. "Treat it like noise," he yelled to Alice. "Like static."

They hurried down the emergency staircase next to the elevator shaft. The sound was less intense here. "Why not take the elevator?" Alice panted.

"Phizwhiz runs the elevator," Vernor replied. "It might not work at all . . . or he might start compensating for all those years of public safety."

As Alice grasped the implication of what Vernor had said, events proved him right. A sudden high-pitched screaming sound shot down past them on the other side of the wall. A heavy crash echoed up the elevator shaft. "We better look out for machines when we get outside," said Vernor.

The square outside the em building was a scene of total chaos. The automated taxis and transport vans were racing around in pursuit of wildly screaming pedestrians.

One could tell they were screaming only by watching their faces, for no sounds could be heard over the incredible blast of electronic madness from the large speakers at every corner. Crushed bodies were strewn about, and many people had fallen from exhaustion or disorientation. The street cleaning robots hurried along the sidewalks, hacking at these people's necks and at the abdomens of those who were still standing.

Vernor watched one young man escape a pursuing taxi by climbing a lamppost; and then, numbed by the blast of sound from the speaker on the lamppost, slide down to rest at its base. The taxi was busy running back and forth over a screaming lady who refused to die, and it seemed that the young man might be safe. But then a trapdoor near the lamppost flew open, a small crab-like vehicle darted out ... and seconds later the young man was slumped over with his throat ripped out.

Phizwhiz was compensating all right. It was fortunate that the world's stockpile of nuclear weapons had been dismantled years ago ... for public safety. Was public safety so bad, after all? Was this horrible and pathetic slaughter preferable to the glazed daze which had preceded it?

Vernor and Alice were still standing on the steps leading down from the em building to the square. A number of people stood with them ... scared to go down into the street and scared to go back into the building ... which seemed to be filling with strong-smelling fumes. Fumigation? A fire?

A heavy van and three taxis came speeding towards the steps. The crowd shrank back up towards the em building, but now cleaning robots were seething out of the building's doors, slashing at everyone within reach. The crowd surged back and forth, trampling several people underfoot.

Alice was pressed against Vernor's chest. She looked up at him. "We did this, Vernor. I want to die."

She twisted out of his grasp and began worming through the crowd, apparently to throw herself to the attacking vehicles below.

Vernor struggled to keep up with her, literally climbing over several people in the way. They reached the bottom perimeter of the crowd on the steps at the same time.

"Wait, Alice. Don't leave me," Vernor shouted over the noise as she hurried into the open. Desperate, he ran after her, caught hold of her, and hoisted her across his shoulders. A taxi was speeding towards them. Vernor took what seemed like the only possible move.

With a sudden twisting motion, he turned and heaved Alice back-first through the taxi's windshield. It shattered into powder and she slid limply into the passenger compartment as the taxi rammed into the backs of Vernor's legs.

He managed to jump up a little, and slid rapidly over the hood and through the smashed-out windshield; but not without slamming his head against a jagged plastic edge.

Since the automatic driver was under the hood with the engine, the taxi's cabin was exclusively for passengers. Alice was lying there unconscious but alive—half on the seat and half on the floor, blood oozing from her parted lips. There was a large gash on the back of Vernor's head, and his shirt was soaked with blood.

The taxi seemed to be aware that it was occupied, although the speaker on the dash emitted only the same blare as all the other speakers under Phizwhiz's control. The taxi stopped trying to run people down and began concentrating on killing Vernor and Alice.

The taxi wove through the surging activity on the square to get to the expressway. Vernor knew what was coming, but it seemed no safer to get out . . . and he couldn't get out anyway, with Alice unconscious and the taxi going faster, faster . . .

They were speeding across a bridge now. At the end of the bridge the road rose up and veered left. The taxi was doing about seventy now, and the wind through the broken windshield beat at Vernor's eyes. It was clear what was going to happen. They were going to shoot up the rise, miss the turn, and crash through the guard rail, cata-pulting through space to what lay below.

Vernor wedged his feet and his left hand against the front of the passenger compartment, and pressed him-self protectively over Alice. He kissed her face again and again, though he didn't want to wake her. Not to this. He glanced back out the open windshield. The guard-rail was upon them. So soon. So terribly soon.

# TWENTY
## wine

The impossibly violent motion through dark space stopped; and Vernor Maxwell was lying in smoking wreckage with a corpse in his arms.

"Alice, oh Alice." Sobs racked his body and he sucked in lungfuls of air; wanting never to stop. He pressed the body closer to him. "Don't leave me here, Alice, don't leave. Let me come with you."

But the reality he was embedded in wasn't finished. Flames licked at his calf, and when he jerked his leg away a terrible pain shot up it, jolting him into physical activity. Alice was dead and he was lying in a slowly burning taxi. Instinct took over, and he obeyed mechanically.

Vernor dragged himself out of the twisted hole where the windshield had been. His left leg was broken. Flames were all over the taxi now. He reached in to drag Alice's body out, but his left leg buckled and he fell to the ground. It was no use. Crawl back in, his mind told him, but his body wouldn't obey. He dragged himself away from the flaming taxi to lean against a plasticrete wall. He began sobbing again as he watched the blackening smoke pour out of the taxi, and after an indefinite period of time he sank into unconsciousness.

He was awakened by someone shaking his shoulder. It was a bum. He realized now that the taxi had crashed into an alley in the Waterfront district. The bum took in Vernor's tearstained face and jerked his head towards the charred wreck of the taxi. "She's gone, friend. You better get on your feet before the machines find you here."

Keeping his head averted lest he see something unbearable, Vernor leaned on the bum's shoulder and started down the alley with him.

"I got a place down by the water," the bum explained. "I was over a few blocks scrounging the restaurants' garbage when the War broke out. Kitchen robot came out after me with a carving knife. I got up on the roofs. Took me four hours just to get back here."

"The War?" Vernor said thickly. He felt so dazed. He reached back to feel the wound on his head.

"I wouldn't touch that if I was you," the bum cautioned, then went on with his story. "Yeah, the War. The machines against the people. Hell, I seen it coming for years. Nobody listened, nobody ever listened to me. I moved down here to get away from people as much as from the machines. I keep the kids away with rocks, the loaches don't bother me, and whenever a clean-up robot decides to evict me I throw it in the river." They were under a ramp leading to the bridge, and the bum stopped. "Here we are."

"The War," Vernor slurred, "it's my fault. I'm the one who gave Phizwhiz free will. But I never thought . . ." He started to weep and sank to the ground.

"Take it easy, buddy. Take it easy." The old man pushed some rags around Vernor. "Give yourself a break." But Vernor was out again.

The next few days passed in a flickering of wakefulness and unconsciousness. It was hard to say which was worse . . . when awake, Vernor had the pain and the awful guilt to contend with, but when he was asleep these elements were incorporated into terrible, merciless visions, unlimited in space and time.

Strange, strange dreams. And it wasn't just the blow on his head, it was something to do with having completed the circuit around Circular Scale. Some strange new dimension had been added to his mind's space, something more than the mere soul which he had promised Phizwhiz.

When Vernor could forget his own feelings he would wonder about Phizwhiz. What had happened? Phizwhiz was certainly alive and conscious, there was no doubt about that, but why had he become so vicious, so malignant? If anything, Vernor felt more passive and gentle than before. Still, the first thing he and Alice had done on their return was to kill three people. Would he have done that before the trip around Circular Scale? Would Alice? Maybe the noise Phizwhiz had been making had made them do it. Blame it on Phizwhiz, sure, but who had changed Phizwhiz? Vernor Maxwell. And why? To make the world dangerous enough to be interesting.

Old Bill, the machine-hating bum who'd rescued Vernor, went out foraging for food every day and brought back daily reports on the War's progress. Certain parts of the City were simply too dangerous to enter—they were populated by fleets of killer machines. In the residential regions, such as Dreamtown and the Waterfront, all the machines had been smashed during the first few days' combat. And active battles were still underway in certain disputed parts of the city.

There were rumors that the surviving Dreamers had organized an army under the leadership of Mick Turner and some of the other Angels. "You're an Angel, aren't you, Vernor?" Old Bill asked one evening, two weeks after the War's outbreak.

"Yeah, I was." Vernor's voice was slurred, but not from the head injury. His wounds were just about healed, though he still had a bad limp. "Gimme that wine."

"You've had enough wine, you. I didn't save your life so you could turn into a bum like me. You're an Angel, not a bum."

Vernor shook his head hopelessly. "I'm not even a bum. If it wasn't for me she'd still be alive." He lurched towards Old Bill menacingly, "I said gimme that wine, old man."

Old Bill surrendered the bottle grudgingly. "There ain't much left." He watched with displeasure as Vernor chugged the rest of it. "Kid, it's about time for you to move on. It's been interesting having you, but you're just about healed up . . . and me, well, you know, I'm a hermit. And I'm damn tired of you hogging so much wine."

"I paid for it, didn't I?" Vernor challenged.

"Sure, sure you paid for it. That ain't the point and you know it. The point's that I'm sick of watching you fall apart. You're body's well now, and the only way your mind is going to heal is for you to *plunge back into the fray*."

"Why don't *you* plunge into the fray?" sneered Vernor.

"This *is* the fray for me. Getting drunk under a bridge. For *you* it's got to be going out and killing off the machines." The old man was right, and Vernor knew it.

"All right," he said, throwing the empty plastic wine bottle high out over the river. "Tomorrow I go kill machines."

"That's my boy," said Old Bill. "Now get some more wine."

Vernor slept badly that night. His last thought before sleeping had been of the instant before the taxi crashed through the guard-rail. In his dream the thought returned to him over and over . . . always in the same way.

He would be floating in a vaguely athletic dream space when it would slowly dawn on him that the random patterns around him were taking on a peculiar significance. As he watched, the space around him would contract and form itself once again into that terrible instant before the taxi crash. "Too soon," he'd think and then force the vision to shrink on down to invisibility, but soon it would have gone around Circular Scale to surround him again with a vast slowly dawning horror . . . which would once again draw itself together to form the unbearable scene . . . which would dwindle again, only to surround him again . . . and again and again, faster and faster . . .

Some time before dawn he jerked up to a sitting position. It was dark under the bridge and the unbearable thought loop was still running in some part of his mind . . . some new part of his mind. He staggered down to the river and splashed water on his face. Slowly the dream faded. It was time to go.

Old Bill was asleep and snoring wetly. Vernor left the rest of his money in the old hermit's pocket and started walking.

He reached the burned taxi just before sunrise. He couldn't quite bring himself to look inside. But he knelt near it and said his last goodbyes to Alice. There was no way to make it right—all those decisions that had ended with her dead like this, instead of on a lovely outing.

He wept softly for awhile, then picked up a tubular length of guard-rail for a crutch, and went on down the alley.

Dawn was breaking now and he saw some people trucking by on a street up ahead. Suddenly eager to re-enter the world, he hurried out to the sidewalk and began limping along after the others, leaning on the staff he'd found near Alice's pyre.

# three blocks

The whole City seemed so different. It was less crowded for one thing—many people had died during the first few days of the War. There were no taxis, vans, or street-cleaning robots moving about, of course; but there were also no radios, no electric lights, no running water. Garbage was piled everywhere; rats and roaches scuttled underfoot. There was no more Dreamfood and people were living on canned goods. Gardens were springing up. On the whole, morale was good, but the outbreak of disease and famine seemed imminent. Some were leaving the City for the countryside, but not many . . . it was, after all, a long trip by foot with the constant threat of machine attack. There was some hope that people would be able to get into and start up the various utility plants, but as yet the Eastside and its factories was still under the machines' control.

Vernor and Alice had seen the galaxy spin yet they'd returned to Earth only a week after leaving it. Vernor still didn't understand how. Time—time was a crazy maelstrom. Sometimes he imagined this was all a hallucination, and that he'd awaken in the scale-ship, still in Alice's arms.

What had become of Professor Kurtowski in his East-side hideout? No telling. But everyone knew about Mick Turner. While Vernor had been gone Mick had been busy organizing an underground network of revolutionaries to strike after Vernor's work with Phizwhiz was completed. They hadn't anticipated that Phizwhiz would turn against the human race, but they'd had the organization to take control of Dreamtown when the War started.

Vernor decided to walk to Dreamtown. He's only need to cross three blocks of machine-controlled territory to get there. He scrounged a meal and set off.

As he neared the machines' turf he saw fewer and fewer people. Finally he was all alone, walking down the middle of a deserted street toward Dreamtown with the aid of his crutch of plastic guardrail.

His partially healed leg was paining him considerably, and a bright mid-morning sun beat down on him. His senses should have been at a high pitch of attention, but somehow he felt drowsy and distant in the hot light.

With the suddenness of a hit of speed, a dog-sized cleaner robot sped out of a small street on his left, broadcasting Phizwhiz's electronic snarl. Vernor turned to face it, holding his staff at the ready. Although he didn't much care if he lived or died, he was eager to fight.

The robot was roughly hemispherical, and was sliding along supported by some type of field. When it was almost upon him, Vernor danced to one side, smashing downwards with his staff at the spot where he'd just been.

The robot, however, wasn't there. It had swerved as quickly as Vernor had moved, and now smashed into his

legs . . . easily toppling him, caught unaware. The robot
scooted up towards Vernor's head, and a cutting arc of
electricity crackled into life between two stubby antennae
on its smooth carapace.

As it moved towards his head the robot passed over his
staff, which was lying on the ground. Vernor seized the
opportunity to lift his end of the stick, tilting the domed
machine up on one edge. Using his hands, Vernor quickly
finished the job of flipping the robot over. Helpless to
right itself, the machine began emitting a distress signal.

His hands slightly numb from the effects of the robot's
support field, Vernor hurried on down the street. Dreamtown was still two blocks away.

The next cross-street was a main thoroughfare, and had
two taxis patrolling it. They spotted Vernor as soon as
he saw them, and accelerated towards him, blaring the
Phizwhiz noise. This was going to be a tough one. If he
could make it past these taxis there'd be maybe another
small robot and then he'd be in Dreamtown. He'd go
to Waxy's and have some weed with Mick—it'd be fine.
With an effort Vernor wrenched his attention back to the
present.

He was running across the intersection toward Dreamtown. The taxis were about twenty feet from him, heading towards him from either side. It looked like the taxi
on the right might reach him first. Even though he wasn't
fully clear on what his strategy was, some instinct told
him to angle to the left.

It was only at the split second when the two taxis were
evenly spaced at arm's length on either side of Vernor that

he consciously understood his plan. Jump! He dug the end of his staff into the street and pole-vaulted.

For an instant he hung some five feet in the air, but that instant was long enough. The taxis, who had perhaps been counting on his body to cushion the blow, smashed into each other at the point where he'd just been. He landed on the hood of one and was thrown off as it spun away from the collision point.

It was quiet. Vernor picked himself up, suddenly feeling the pain in his leg again as the adrenalin faded. Limping badly, he retrieved his staff from the taxi's wreckage. "Thanks, Alice," he said softly.

One more small street and he'd be in Dreamtown. He could even see a person two blocks ahead. But there was bound to be a fucking robot patrolling that one small street in between. His leg was hurting badly and he was tired. Better not rest, there'd be more taxis coming, or maybe even a van. He shuffled forward, leaning heavily on his length of guard-rail.

There was indeed a repair robot patrolling the last street he had to cross. Vernor hugged a wall and peered around the corner, watching the robot's movements. When it seemed to be as far away as it was likely to get, he set off across the intersection with an uneven trot.

Quickly the machine spotted him came after him. Vernor felt tired and dizzy, but he beat the repair robot across the narrow street. He went into the next block and leaned, panting, against a building, unable to run further just now.

To his right Vernor could see Dreamtown. He recognized a few buildings and now he could actually see several people, although the closest was over a block away. To his left was the corner around which the repair robot would inevitably come. He raised his crutch and poised himself to smash the machine when it appeared.

With a sudden blast of noise it was upon him. This one was bigger than the first one, and had a nasty-looking set of tools projecting from its shell. Vernor connected with the machine's prismed photo-cells, breaking one.

Using a pincer-like appendage, the robot plucked the staff from Vernor's grasp before he could raise it to strike again. The staff clattered into the street and the robot backed up, then charged. Vernor was ready, and did a bull-fight number, sidestepping the machine at the last instant.

But now the only option was flight. He started running at top speed for Dreamtown. Suddenly his left leg gave out and he fell. The robot caught up rapidly and stopped next to Vernor's head.

A wicked metal cutting edge struck at his throat, but he managed to catch and hold the mechanical arm. Another arm, bearing a screw-driver end, appeared and began hacking away. He fended it off as well as he could, but it was making deep cuts in both his arms. Finally the robot wrenched the cutting blade free of Vernor's grasp.

He sank back with a sigh. This was it. The blade came angling towards his neck and . . .

Stopped. There was a sizzling sound from a bright hole which had appeared in the robot's shell. A laser beam. Someone had shot the robot.

Strong hands helped Vernor to his feet. "You must want

to get to Dreamtown pretty bad," said a woman's voice. Vernor turned to see her.

"Oily Allie!" he exclaimed.

"Vernor! We've been waiting for you." Allie pulled him to his feet and patted him on the back. As always, her dark, greasy hair was a tangle of spikes. "Wait till Mick sees you!"

They started towards Dreamtown, Vernor leaning heavily on Oily Allie. "Yeah, we got a sort of border patrol here," Allie explained. "Otherwise Phizwhiz'd be chipping away at our territory. Usually we don't rescue people, but after I saw the job you did on the taxis it seemed like a shame to let that one little robot finish you off. I hadn't even recognized you. Good thing I saved you. You're a hero, Vernor."

"For what?" Vernor asked weakly. His arms were bleeding badly and his leg seemed to be completely broken again.

"For what?" Allie repeated. "For what? For making Phizwhiz go nuts! Sure some people miss the old life, watching Hollows all day long, but I love it like this." To demonstrate, Oily Allie spun around and blasted the lifeless robot again with the heavy laser she cradled with her right arm. "Ftoom!" said Allie.

For an instant Vernor's weight was on his broken leg. An explosion went off behind his eyeballs and he fainted.

When he awoke he was on a bed. It was dark, and a young woman was sitting near him. His wounds had been dressed and his leg was in a casing of rigid plastic foam. He felt pretty good.

"Where am I?" he asked.

"Hi," said the young woman. "You're about two blocks from where you collapsed. Allie brought you and we fixed you up. Do you want some food?" She offered him a tube of Dreamfood. Green. Aaaahh.

After eating Vernor sat up. "What time is it?"

"About nine. You've been out since noon." She was pretty. He tried to get up, but she pushed him back. "Stay here. Allie will come for you in the morning. You need more rest."

"Okay," he said, relaxing back towards sleep. His last thought was a sense of gratitude that he felt well enough to want to fuck his nurse.

That night Vernor dreamed of swimming in a phosphorescent sea. There was a group of fish chasing each other in a circle. Each fish was bigger than the next. Each fish had its mouth open to swallow the one in front of it, and each was swimming rapidly away from the open mouth snapping at its tail.

The speed of the Circular Scale increased. Finally there was an articulated gulp as each of the fish was swallowed by the one behind it. And then silence.

Vernor was alone, drifting amorphous in the peaceful sea.

# TWENTY-TWO

# together

In the morning, the nurse cut the cast off Vernor's leg. Yesterday she'd injected some glue into the break; the cast had been to hold his leg still while the glue set. His arm wounds had been coated with plastic skin, and he'd been shot full of vitamins and antibiotics. He felt like a new man.

Oily Allie showed up late in the morning to take him to Waxy's. It was a distance of several miles, and what with stopping to rest and greet old friends it was afternoon before they made it to the Angels' headquarters.

Mick Turner met them at the door. "Vernor Max!" he shouted happily, embracing him. "Man, everything is gonna be great! Come on, let's smoke some shit!"

They sat down at a table. The place was crowded with Angels. They welcomed Vernor like a hero. "How did you all get out of jail?" Vernor asked.

"You ought to know, dad, you're the one that got Phizwhiz to open all the doors," answered an Angel named Leroy.

Open the jail's doors? Sure, it stood to reason that when Phizwhiz started his war against the humans he would release what he still thought of as the most destructive members of society. He had been too naive, however, to realize that exactly those people who'd been destructive to the old society might be the new society's most valuable asset in the War.

"So all the Angels are here?" Vernor asked Mick, looking around the room.

"Most of 'em," Mick answered. "Some are out on patrol. Some are dead. Moto-O got it yesterday trying to bomb the em building . . . I'm sorry I couldn't come get you with Oily this morning. I had to get today's fighting organized."

"General Mick?" Vernor smiled. There were a large number of weapons about . . . battery operated lasers with the governors replaced by amplifiers, antimatter bombs of Oily Allie's design, spray-guns loaded with a solvent to dissolve the robots' shells . . . and even a few antique bazookas and flame-throwers looted from the museum.

The Angels were crowding around Vernor shouting questions. How had he done it? What should they do next? Where was the Professor? Could he make Phizwhiz start the factories up again? It was too much at once, and he just grinned.

"He's half-dead," Mick yelled. "Go out on your patrols. Vernor and me'll get the act together and tonight we'll lay it down."

Singly and in groups the Angels left, and soon the bar had quieted. Mick lit a stick of seeweed, inhaled, passed it to Vernor. "So what happened?"

"What happened? You know. It's hard to say. Alice is dead." Vernor stopped and drew on the joint.

"Alice? That's terrible. She was with you?"

"Yeah, I got Burke to bring the scale-ship over to the em building and he let Alice come to live with me. We hooked Phizwhiz into some sensors on the ship and then we took the big trip. Circular Scale."

"So it really is circular? Wait till you tell Kurtowski."

"Yeah. We gotta find him. Do you know where he is for sure, Mick?"

"Naw. We haven't been able to get over there. To the Eastside. But he's probably still in that hide-out. Waiting for the Revolution." Mick shook his head. "We got it all. And more. But—the robots killed Alice?"

"Yeah," muttered Vernor. "My fault."

Mick pulled on his reefer, studying the smoke. "But there was no problem getting back to Earth?"

"Are you kidding? I have no idea why it worked. It wasn't just the machine. It was something we did with our heads, our bodies ... Alice and me—" He broke off, filled by the memory of that last star-fuck with Alice. "Didn't you see us?"

"See you? How ... wait, you mean that was you and Alice in the sky? Just before the War? Lot of people saw that, but nobody's sure they did. You know. I'd thought it was a Hollow that Phizwhiz sent out just before ..." Turner stopped. "I didn't see it myself. I know a girl who did. Ramona. She liked your prong." The callous Mick chuckled, forgetting about Alice. "Go on."

"Well, my idea had been that putting this scale loop into Phizwhiz would provide a nexus for paradox—a soul. And I figured once he had a soul he'd want to be friends with the first person he talked to."

"Which was going to be you."

"Which *was* me. Only just because he had a soul didn't mean he was going to be a regular guy . . . which was something that hadn't occurred to me."

"What'd he say?" Mick asked.

"I don't know. It was like this mystical stuff and then he started in on how I couldn't understand, though actually I *was* following him . . . but then he got real snotty and said he wasn't going to work for people anymore. And that was about it."

"So he started playing a chaos soundtrack and stomping us," Mick finished. "It must have been a pretty bad scene up by the em building. Lot of machines up there. You're the only guy I've met who made it out, actually."

"Yeah, it was bad," Vernor said slowly. "I threw Alice into a taxi and climbed in. It took off and crashed near the waterfront. And that's when she died." He inhaled some more smoke. "I feel bad about what I started. I mean, seeing all those people get killed and then Alice . . . like most of the time I wish I was dead." He smiled, embarrassed.

"From what Oily Allie told me about yesterday, you don't act like a man who wishes he was dead." Mick leaned across the table. "You're a killer, Vernor. So am I. We can *live* with the world like this. I'm not talking about Alice here, but most of those people that got it that first day didn't even know they were alive . . . watching Hollows, taking tranks, doing what Us said . . . fuck. It's *our* turn now."

Vernor remembered how the man by the lamppost had looked just before the robot ripped out his throat. "I understand what you're saying, Mick. I understand it, but seeing it happen is something different." He was quiet for awhile. It was comfortable here in Waxy's with the death and fighting far away. There was a pleasant yellow thickness to the air. He felt like he was outside himself. He could see all his feelings and emotions at once, like a landscape. No secrets. There he was. So? Sure, sure he'd keep living. It was sad ... but there it was. "What happens next?" he said finally.

"Right now the problem is survival," Mick answered. "Phizwhiz did everything we'd hoped to do with the Revolution ... everyone's out of jail, all the big Users and loaches uptown are dead, there's no public safety by a long shot. People don't expect the machines to live their lives anymore. The Revolution is here ... all we have to do is live long enough to enjoy it. First thing is to get the basic stuff going again. Food, water, electricity, sewers. We'll need organization. Everyone working together."

Vernor smiled. "You sound like the Governor himself, Mick."

"But this is *real*, man. Before, there wasn't anybody had to do anything. As long as we have real jobs to do, we can groove."

"What happens when you get all the factories running again?" probed Vernor. "What's there going to be to do then?"

"For one thing we're not going back to everything being run automatic. For another ... we're going to the stars." Mick looked as inspirational as Vernor had ever seen him. "The stars, Vernor. That's what was missing before—a frontier. There's bound to be some way to use the VFG to get us anywhere we want to go."

Mick was right. Space exploration had been dead for years. They'd sent a few squares out to the planets and back ... and that was it. People lost interest in it. One of these astronaut types would come back from Mars ... "How was it, Colonel?" "Well, Mr. Straight, it was unpleasant. We forgot to bring steak with us and the lighting was poor. I wasn't able to shave for two weeks. My principal feeling when I stepped onto that planet was one of gratitude to the Us government for making this possible. We saluted the flag there, although the dust storms made it difficult. On the whole I'd say that it was worthwhile sending me, since I've gotten so much pussy ever since my return." "Thank you, Colonel."

The promise of the stars had seemed permanently out of mankind's reach. The technology may have been there, but the government was not willing to take the risks. But now the government was gone ... with the vFG, all you'd need was to be knocked off course a little and you could come back anywhere. Anywhere you dreamed. "I'm with you, Mick," said Vernor.

Mick grinned. "The gang is trying to cut Phizwhiz's cables to the Eastside today. Maybe it'll be safe to go over and see the Professor tomorrow."

Most of the Angels returned around supper time. Waxy's was a sort of co-ed officer's club now ... the Angels being the leaders of Mick's army. The day's actions had been successful. Phizwhiz's main cable to the Eastside ran under the moving sidewalk in the walktube. The Angels and their collaborators had fought their way down to the sidewalk. There had been massed attacks by the many repair robots in the walktube, but the machines had, after all, not been designed for fighting, and they'd soon been knocked out.

A number of men and women had been whisked away to probable death when Phizwhiz had suddenly started the sidewalk rolling at top speed, but the remaining troops had managed to pry up a large piece of the sidewalk. Underneath they'd found a coaxial cable some two feet across, and the rest of the day had been devoted to cutting through it with lasers. Periodically machines had come hurtling down the walktube towards them, but, in the end, the cable had been fully severed.

The problem now was going to be to keep Phizwhiz's robots from repairing the cable break. A barrier and a large group of armed men and women had been left there to prevent this. For now, though, Phizwhiz no longer controlled the Eastside.

This meant that it would be safe to enter the waterworks, the sewage plant, the hydroponic farm, the cloning center—and try to get them running again. There would, of course, be the microwave-controlled repair robots to contend with, but the threat they posed was limited in comparison to that of a whole factory. Also, several detachments of men were planning to knock out Phizwhiz's microwave antennae the next day.

Taking and holding the Eastside was important not only because of the utilities, but because the robot factories were there . . . and they'd been running around the clock. The speculation was that Phizwhiz was designing and building specially designed killer machines which would be less vulnerable and more deadly than the taxis and the repair robots. But now the production of killer robots had been halted by the cutting of the control cable.

The mood in Waxy's was one of elation over the day's success and Vernor's return. Toast after toast was drunk, smoked, injected, and snorted. Soon, the room seemed like a solid hypercube of four-dimensional spacetime, so distinctly did Vernor see the trails of moving objects.

Mick was standing in front of him with a pornographically sexy girl. "This is Ramona," Mick said. "Who saw you up in the sky."

Sky? With A—put that away. "How'd I look," said Vernor.

"Astral," she answered, nudging him with her breast.

"I'm strictly gross material plane, darling," Vernor answered, squeezing her bottom, whose cheeks were exposed by a cut-out in her tight pants. "Oh, you feel so lush and ripe."

Ramona smiled and kissed him, pushing her tongue lazily against his. With a gentle, knowing hand, she felt his crotch. "Last time I saw this thing, it looked like Florida."

# in the sky

Vernor and Ramona had a good time with each other in Vernor's room above the barroom at Waxy's. When he awoke, she was gone, and he could hear voices downstairs.

He went down to find Mick and Oily Allie. "You smell *good*, Vernor," Mick said leaning close and sniffing him. "I hope you didn't make Ramona do nothing she never done before."

"That might be hard," said Oily Allie. She was wearing ragged jeans and a stained black T-shirt showing off her muscular arms.

"Is there any food?" asked Vernor. The Dreamfood taps still worked, but the food which came out was poisoned, natch.

Mick reached into a crate behind the bar. "We've got some vintage tubes. Green?"

"Green." Vernor squeezed down the paste. "So, are we going to find the Professor today?"

"Today's the day," Oily Allie responded, picking up her laser and patting it. "Not many folks can handle this baby," she said proudly. Indeed the laser must have weighed seventy pounds. Allie had stolen it from a taxi factory where she worked before the War. It had been used to cut thick sheets of plastic in the factory, but the ingenious Allie had turned it into a highly effective weapon.

"Right," Mick said. "You and me and Oily Allie are going into the Eastside to the Professor's warehouse."

"What about all the vans and robots?" Vernor asked. "Maybe it would be wise to wait until the microwave towers are down."

Mick looked unconcerned. "Ah, we'll just keep off the streets. Stay high, ya dig?"

"You're the General," Vernor answered.

Allie gave Vernor a backpack which she said would be helpful, and then they set off for the Eastside.

Vernor felt a little dazed from all the drugs he had taken the night before. He was still having his looping dreams . . . where a thought would seem to travel around some internal Circular Scale loop of his all night . . . now shrinking down out of his consciousness, now slowly gathering itself in his mind from every direction. It was not necessarily unpleasant to loop something all night. Last night, for instance, it had been the taste of Ramona's two-tone kisses.

The trip around Circular Scale had definitely altered his mind. Not only were there these strange looping dreams, there were unexpected thoughts which would arise full-blown. Where, for instance, had the idea of vaulting above the taxis' point of impact come from? He hadn't known he was planning to do that until it was over.

It was not just that he was having more thoughts, some of his thoughts seemed to have no logical connection with his usual thoughts.

They were approaching the region where Dreamtown shaded into the Eastside. There were fewer and fewer people to be seen, and after Oily Allie had blasted two robots and a taxi they knew they'd entered Phizwhiz's turf.

"How far do you figure it is from here, Vernor?" Mick asked.

"Twenty blocks at least."

Oily Allie made a brief mental calculation. "We better hit the sky. If we stay down here it's going to take about three blasts a block to handle the robots." She patted her laser. "The charge on this laser's only good for thirty blasts."

There were still some apartment buildings on this street. They entered one and climbed the stairs to the flat roof. Most of the buildings in this part of the Eastside were about the same height, and it wouldn't have been too difficult to simply walk the twenty blocks by moving from roof to roof—that is if there had not been streets and alleys separating the buildings. As it was, they were able to walk about fifty yards until they came to a gap of some thirty feet between roofs.

Vernor leaned over and looked down. They were seven stories up. There was a small street down there with a few idling robots.

"Well, gang," he said. "Maybe Mick can jump that, but think of poor Allie here with that heavy laser, and me with my backpack . . ." Mick and Allie didn't seem to be listening.

Vernor was alarmed. "Are you two nuts? Jump thirty feet? Are we going to leave all our stuff here? And even if we do, I really don't . . ."

Mick glanced over. "Come on, Vernor, cut the shit. Get the gear out of your pack. Oily Allie's built us three flying machines."

Oily Allie, a mad Marie Curie of the times, had been fond of building various unsafe gadgets out of odds and ends which she stole from her factory in the pre-War days. Vernor remembered now that Allie had built some sort of personal rocket which she tested in the park at night—but surely not under such stringent conditions as jumping thirty feet between two seven-story buildings.

Vernor opened his pack. It contained a number of tubes, some of which seemed to be hissing. Oily Allie quickly snapped the tubes together until she had three T's. One for each of them. On each T, the upright was a tube about four feet long and three inches in diameter; it had small vents on the sides, an adjustable diaphragm closing one end, and a solid cross-bar attached to the other end.

"Not a very hefty rocket," ventured Vernor.

"Doesn't have to be," Oily Allie beamed. "And rocket ain't really the right word. It's an anti-rocket. It sucks. Show him, Mick."

Mick stuck the upright of the T out between his legs, with the cross-bar behind him. He was sitting on the cross-bar and the diaphragm end of the vented tube was sticking up at the sky. He reached up and moved a lever to open a tiny hole in the diaphragm closing off the top end of the tube.

The tube jerked up to a vertical position and slowly lifted Mick upwards. When he was some twenty feet above them he pushed forward on the big tube with his hands and back on the cross-bar with his thighs so that the power tube was no longer vertical. It continued drawing him up, but now at an angle. Soon Turner was over the roof on the other side of the street. He let the power tube return to the vertical, adjusted the diaphragm to a pinhole opening, and floated down to the roof on the other side of the street. Grinning, he looked across at Vernor and gave him the finger.

"Get it?" Oily Allie asked. "This lever opens and closes the hole at the top. The air gets sucked in there and the sucking lifts you. That's all there is to it." Allie paused to mount her anti-rocket. "Would you believe those wimps at the factory were using these things to run a fucking ventilation system?"

"How does it work?" Vernor asked, fascinated. "What does the sucking?"

"I've got a tiny black hole mounted in there," Allie explained. "Matter just disappears into it. This little piggie could soak up the whole atmosphere in a couple thousand years."

Vernor wanted to ask more questions, but some roofing robots were approaching them. He mounted his cross-bar. "Easy on that control," Allie shouted, but too late.

In his unfamiliarity with the lever's sensitivity, Vernor had opened the aperture in the top end of the power-tube much too far. He shot upwards to a height of a hundred yards above the roof tops before he managed to stop the aperture down.

Mick was a tiny figure on the roof across the street, and Allie was at the top of a practiced parabola which would land her next to Turner in seconds. Vernor, however, was falling like a stone towards the robot on the roof below him.

He tried to ease the tube's hole open just a little, but again he overdid it, blasting up to a position much higher than his original position. This time, instead of completely closing the opening he managed to leave a hole just large enough to balance his weight.

He was sitting there on his T-bar, hugging the power tube, many hundreds of yards above street-level. Mick and Allie appeared to be doubled over with laughter, though it was hard to tell from so great a distance. Fuck 'em.

His tense muscles relaxed a little and he was able to look around. He had a great view in all directions. Ahead lay the Eastside, factories and warehouses of various shapes jammed together like the tubes in an antique radio. The urban residential districts lay behind him ... on the left Dreamtown with its high-rises; and on the right the Waterfront district where the factory workers lived.

By craning hard he could make out the ribbon of the river through the buildings of the Waterfront; and beyond the river rose the towers of the business district. There was nothing but air between him and the em building, some five miles away.

He could make out the bands and patches of tract homes ringed around these urban districts. They stretched on mile after mile ... a suburban sea dotted here and there with other urban centers. The City.

It was so *big*. Sure they might be able to organize the Dreamtown of one center ... but the rest? Let it be, a voice in Vernor's mind seemed to say, you don't *have* to organize other people's lives. *But what if they're assholes?* he asked. And what if *you* are, the voice answered.

A slight breeze had carried him to a position over the block of roofs where Mick and Allie were. Cautiously, Vernor closed the tube opening a little more, and he drifted down.

## TWENTY-FOUR

# room

**V**ernor's handling of his anti-rocket ... actually Oily Allie called it a sky-sucker ... grew smoother, and soon the three of them were hopping several blocks at a time together.

"What's the highest you've gone?" Vernor asked Allie during one such hop. The sky-suckers operated soundlessly, except for the rushing of the air into the tube, so it was easy to talk.

"Up past the clouds a couple of times," Allie answered. "Gets cold up there, though. Windy, too. One time I got all screwed up inside a cloud and came out headed straight down at top speed." Oily Allie chuckled, "The G's snapped the T-bar off when I pulled back up ... I was hugging the power tube for what they call dear life. My hands were slipping and I couldn't reach the control—"

Vernor had suddenly lost interest in this conversation, and he began scanning the buildings ahead. "There's the plastics factory, Mick," he shouted.

"Yeah. Let's land there and get our bearings."

They landed on the barrel-vaulted roof of the factory. They could hear robots moving about inside. "There's the street the loach coach was driving us on after our scale trip," said Mick, pointing.

Vernor nodded, and they began hopping along the roofs of the buildings lining the street in question. Soon they were above the spot where Kurtowski's bomb had scarred the street's surface. And there was the alley where they'd crawled through the little hole.

One last hop with the sky-suckers and they were on top of the warehouse containing the Professor's hide-out. "Should we blast in through the front door?" suggested Vernor.

"Better not," Mick answered. "He might want to keep using that door. Let's go in through the roof. Allie?"

Oily Allie hefted her laser doubtfully. "It'll take a lot of power. I'll have to run it continuous for a couple of minutes to cut a hole big enough for us."

"Shit, man, we're not going to have to blast any more robots," Mick responded. "Anything hassles us we just turn on the sky-suckers and we're gone."

"Okay," Allie said, switching on the heavy industrial laser. At full power, it was able to cut a circle through the roof's material in a matter of minutes, although the beam seemed noticeably weaker by the time the cut-out disk of roof crashed down into the warehouse.

They peered in. It was indeed the right place.

"Hey, Professor," Vernor yelled, but only echoes answered him.

"His room's soundproofed," Mick pointed out.

"Oh, yeah," Vernor answered. "Well, let's float down on the sky-suckers."

Moments later the three of them were in the aisles of the gloomy warehouse, lit only by the sun streaming in through the hole in the roof sixty feet above them. The fifty foot mounds of crates surrounded them as before.

"I think it was down this way," Vernor said, heading down one of the aisles. Mick and Oily Allie followed him for about twenty yards, and he stopped, "I don't know, maybe it was—"

He was interrupted by a sudden blare of noise. A gigantic forklift was rumbling down the aisle after them. Allie whirled and blasted at it with her laser, but the machine was so huge, and the laser beam so weakened, that the blasts had no effect. Quickly they rose to the roof on their sky-suckers.

At first it seemed that they were out of the machine's reach, but then the prongs of the colossal forklift reared up to some three feet below the flat ceiling. The machine rushed murderously towards them. There was no hope of out-maneuvering it with the sky-suckers, which were designed for up and down movement in open spaces. Quickly they scrambled to safety on the top of one of the stacks of crates, cutting the sky-suckers' power.

The top of the stack was a fifty-foot square, so as long as they kept back from the edges they were safe from the forklift.

"We got to get back out that hole and wait for them to knock out the microwave towers," Oily Allie said. "Thing to do is jump off the other side of the stack and sneak on around that metal mother."

Almost as if it had heard him, the forklift took three crates from one side of the pile on which they were crouching, backed up to a position under the hole they'd cut and forced the crates up so that the top one became wedged in their exit hole.

"What a fucking drag," Mick said, punctuating their stunned silence. The forklift returned and began methodically demolishing their stack; carrying boxes from it to add to one of the other stacks with tireless, mindless industry.

When their stack of crates had been whittled down to the thickness of a few boxes, they jumped down on the opposite side; cushioning the fall with the sky-suckers, which they then used to pull themselves up to the top of the next stack. The machine finished stowing away the crates that remained in the old stack, and then set to work whittling down their new territory.

"And you see what it's doing?" Vernor asked. "It's going to make a solid block of all the crates at the other end of the warehouse so it can chase us around this end."

"This is just really dumb," Oily Allie complained. "I mean if it was really important to me I could probably blast that crate out of the hole."

"Pretend it's really important to you, Allie," suggested Vernor. She aimed the laser and pressed the blast button. The corner of the box charred slightly before the laser finally gave out.

The forklift transferred another load of crates—and the badness of the situation became acute. The new gap in the crate-piles revealed Professor Kurtowski, sitting in an armchair reading a book.

"Look out, Professor!" Vernor yelled, jumping down to his rescue. The forklift tooled forward at the same instant and bumped Vernor with one of its prongs. He'd been leaning down to make a daring Douglas Fairbanks snatch-up of the Professor and was consequently knocked off his T-bar. The sky-sucker shot up to the ceiling and Vernor fell into Kurtowski's lap. Triumphantly, the prongs of the forklift came plummeting down at them. Vernor glanced quickly at the Professor's face to see how the wisest man he knew would meet death.

"That's *quite* enough, Vernor," Kurtowski said, standing up and dumping Vernor onto the floor with a baffled expression.

"Look out!" Vernor screamed, cowering on the floor as he tensed himself for the splat of the prong on Kurtowski's head. But there was no splat.

There was silence, broken finally by Oily Allie shrieking, "Run, Vernor, run!" then breaking into helpless laughter. The forklift had stopped working.

Vernor stood up. "I guess they finally knocked out those microwave antennas," he explained sheepishly to no one in particular. The Professor was standing in front of him looking from Vernor to the forklift to Mick and Oily Allie, fifty feet above them. Finally he smiled at Vernor.

"And you took Phizwhiz for a ride?" he asked.

"Yeah," said Vernor. "We shrank all the way around Circular Scale. What's been bothering me is how did I manage to come back now instead of the future? I mean when we were half the size of the universe, a second of our time was like a billion years Earth time. But here I am."

"That's a good one," said Kurtowski. "What else?"

"I'm wondering about what adding the scale loop might have done to my mind," responded Vernor. "It gave Phizwhiz a soul, or free will, or *some*thing. But I can't quite figure out what it's done to *me*."

"Maybe you should ask Phizwhiz," the Professor replied.

"He doesn't talk anymore," Vernor protested. "He just sends out this sort of loud static. Anyway, *you're* the one to ask."

Kurtowski shrugged. "We can work on it. You need your own answers, though, not mine." He gathered up some papers, then shouted up to the others, "If the local robots aren't working, out let's go over to my lab. I've been in here for weeks. Every time I try to go anywhere some machine tries to kill me. This represents, in my opinion, only a slight improvement over having them try to jail me for my own safety."

# TWENTY-FIVE

# high splits

The trip to Kurtowski's lab was without incident. With the coaxial cables and the microwave towers knocked out, the machines on the Eastside were no longer possessed by a malignant intelligence . . . they were simply machines.

The loaches had left most of the apparatus in the laboratory untouched, and Oily Allie was like a kid in a toy store. She soon settled down to fool with the Professor's matter degenerator, a device which made small black holes. You threw whatever was handy into the hopper, switched on the power and WHAM . . . gravitational collapse would hit whatever you'd thrown in. All the props which hold matter "up" would be knocked out, leaving the mutual gravitational attraction of the mass particles as the only operative force.

The end-result of gravitational collapse is a singular point in the spacetime manifold, inevitably veiled by a dark sphere—our friend the black hole. Although the notion of star-sized black holes in outer space was commonplace, it had only been a few years since Kurtowski's experiments had led to the laboratory creation of small and relatively stable black holes, such as those which powered Oily Allie's sky-suckers.

Oily Allie was delighted to have the opportunity to monkey with the machine which produced these small black holes. She was trying to figure out how to turn it into a portable weapon ... enclosing your antagonists inside a one-way event horizon would certainly be an efficacious way of getting them off your back.

Mick had settled down to another session with the music of the spheres. He'd cranked the galactic signal analyzer to full, and crouched near the machine with the earphones on, occasionally exclaiming when he recognized something he'd seen from the scale-ship.

Vernor and the Professor sat on a battered couch near where the VFG had been before the loaches took it to the em building. "Vernor," Kurtowski was saying, "I might as well tell you, I have no idea what the VFG *really* does."

"It makes things shrink," Vernor answered.

"Ja, but what is shrinking? There are many ways of looking at it. A viewpoint which does not seem unreasonable to me is that the shrinking is accomplished by moving in a direction perpendicular to every direction we can point to in our three-dimensional space. You get smaller because you are *further away*."

Vernor looked puzzled and the Professor tried again. "If you are looking through a window, and you see a man getting much smaller, what do you conclude?"

"That he's walking away from the window."

"Right. My idea is that our three-dimensional space is a window on four-dimensional space. When the VFG makes something shrink in our 'window,' it is doing this by moving it away in the direction of a fourth dimension."

There was a peevish moan from Oily Allie, followed by a high singing note that faded into silence. "Shit," said Allie quietly.

The Professor chuckled appreciatively. "What happened?" asked Vernor.

"I dropped one through the floor," Allie responded.

"Dropped what?" Vernor said, going over to see. It looked as if someone had drilled a hole in the floor next to Allie's boot.

"I made this little tiny black hole and tried to move it with the magnetic clamp, but it slipped," she said, running her hand through her tangled hair. There seemed to be nothing which would prevent the black hole from eating its way straight through the Earth and back again. Anything which it touched would disappear into the singularity at the center.

"Is this going to screw things really bad?" Allie called to Professor Kurtowski.

"No, no," said the Professor. "It's got a built-in instability. It'll pop before it eats more than a few kilotons. Try dropping it on your foot next time."

The crisis over, Vernor returned to the couch and Allie began playing again, but this time with an exaggerated caution.

"About what you were just saying," Vernor resumed. "The VFG made me shrink by moving me in a direction perpendicular to our spacetime? That would fit in with Circular Scale if that new direction was bent into a huge circle."

The Professor was quiet for a few minutes, then finally answered, "Look, Vernor, what makes you so sure that you returned to the same Earth which you left from?"

"There's only one Earth, Professor, and this is it," replied Vernor.

"That's only what you think. Remember how the electron cloud looked to you?"

Mick had finished listening to the space music, and had ambled over to sit on a chair near them. "I remember that," he interjected. "It looked like you *thought* it looked."

"That's right," the Professor responded. "There is, at certain levels, no objective external reality. There is only a probability function which interacts with your brainstates to produce illusions."

"But wait," Vernor protested. "The one thing that I see is what the real thing is. For me anyway." He didn't like this line of thought.

"But imagine that someone was observing *you*, Vernor. Perhaps you would have the appearance of existing in many simultaneous states." The Professor peered at Vernor comically. "Remember that the world you find yourself in now was found at a level *below* the atomic level."

"Remember all those different hyperspheres?" Mick put in. "He's saying that each one of them was an alternate universe!"

The Professor nodded. "Floating in Hilbert space. And . . . since they were shiny, there was an image of you in each of them."

"Hold on," Vernor interrupted. "Are you saying I came back in many different universes at once? Why do I just see one?"

"You just *think* this is the only one," the Professor explained. "But you think that in all the others, too."

Vernor felt confused. "Then what are you guys doing here? I mean if this isn't the same Earth that I left how did you get here?"

"Our brain states, my dear Vernor, are coupled," the Professor responded, waving his hand back and forth between their three heads. "As was borne in upon me when you dropped into my lap back in the warehouse. I was alone in there for two weeks, you know."

"Getting uncoupled," Mick suggested.

The Professor nodded. "I had always believed in principle that I exist in many parallel worlds, but by the end of those two weeks, I . . ." He broke off with a smile, then turned to Vernor. "This is *your* dream, Vernor, are you ready to wake up?"

A chasm seemed to open up around Vernor. For an instant he forgot the names of the things around him. He lost the internal monologue by which external reality is kept unique. There was no feeling of panic, rather an immense feeling of freedom.

An object moved towards him, and he SPLIT took-it/ didn't-take-it, he SPLIT blinked/stared, and he SPLIT talked/kept-silent. Which?

In some world he was saying, "Do you feel this way all the time?" to a Professor Kurtowski who responded with . . . what? Every possible answer.

"How do you ever get anything done?" Vernor continued, and received another infinite response, perfectly tailored to the endless nuances that his question took on.

"It takes care of itself . . ." Mick Turner was saying when

SNAP, Vernor was back to single vision. Mick and the Professor were on the couch and he was sitting on a chair near them, holding a reefer. Vernor opened his mouth, then closed it.

"So you see," the Professor continued. "It is not at all certain that your trip consisted of going around a circle of scale. I am inclined to think, rather, that what you did was jump out of one window and into another."

"And that would explain why I didn't end up a billion years in the future?" Vernor asked slowly.

"You may have jumped out the window, but you kept your glasses on," Mick suggested with mock sincerity.

"But, dammit, I saw how I went around the Circular Scale," Vernor repeated. "That's the way the universe *should* be made, anyhow. No matter, just form. No big and no small . . . every level is right in the middle. A galaxy, a person, and an atom are equally important. A billion years fit inside a nanosecond."

"It's a nice universe, Vernor," the Professor said kindly. "It's just not the only one. But you're right. For you, for all of our brain-states coupled together here, scale is circular. Fine. *As above, so below.*"

There was a loud crash and Oily Allie hollered, "Duck!" Vernor turned to see a deeply black ball flying across the room towards his chest. He hit the floor and the object sailed over him, passing through the wall on the other side of the room without slowing down.

"Allie," the Professor said. "You're a walking, talking argument for the revival of the public safety movement."

"That's how we can kill off Phizwhiz," Allie was saying as she walked over. "Just lob black holes through him."

Vernor felt the justifiable annoyance of one who has narrowly escaped being killed. "Phizwhiz consists of about three-hundred linked installations all over the world, you fucking moron."

Oily Allie was unperturbed. "So, we just stand here and throw the black holes in the right direction about three-hundred times."

"And people who happen to be in the way?" Vernor demanded. "It's just too bad for them?"

"Eventually, we're all losers," said Mick with a shrug.

"It's a moot point, Allie," opined the Professor. "It wouldn't be practical to aim with sufficient accuracy. In any case, I've thought of a better way to handle Phizwhiz." He stared at Vernor.

"Don't tell me, let me guess," Vernor said heatedly. "I'm supposed to go back to the em building and make friends with him even though he wants to kill everyone he sees."

"You don't have to go all the way in there," Mick said soothingly. "There's a terminal in Dreamtown. You and Phizwhiz could probably really get it on talking about your trip."

"But he *doesn't* talk anymore," Vernor protested.

"So plug in," the Professor said simply. Plug in. Vernor fingered the socket at the base of his skull.

"Sure," he said acidly, "plug my brain into a machine whose express purpose is to kill off the human race. That's really a great idea, Professor K."

But Oily Allie was taken by the proposal. "Shit, Vern, we can put in an impedance block to step down the power surge in case he tries to fry you. You'll be as safe as any of us was in the old days. A heavy guy like you should be able to handle anything, as long as we keep the voltage down."

They were all looking at him. Vernor took a large hit off the reefer Mick handed him. "Why not sneeze, Rrose Sélavy?" he murmured, lifting a line from Dadaism. Out loud he said, "Ask me again in the morning."

## TWENTY-SIX
# the one and the many

Somehow no one bothered asking Vernor again in the morning. When he woke up, Allie had already left for Dreamtown to get the terminal rigged up. The plan was for Mick to stay in the lab so that Professor Kurtowski could use his sky-sucker to accompany Vernor to Dreamtown.

"I'll be watching, man," Mick said, flicking on a Hollow receiver in the corner of the room. The familiar electronic brain-jamming sound of the new Phizwhiz filled the room, and matching 3D images danced around the Hollow receiver—a writhing swirl of algorithmic shapes encrusted by fragmentary Hollows of real-world objects . . . ferns, faces, bricks, claws, flames . . . Vernor couldn't look at the display for long without feeling dizzy.

"I'd plug in myself," Kurtowski was saying, "but I don't have a socket. Anyway, you're the one who was with Phizwhiz when he changed, Vernor. Who knows, he may be glad to see you."

They started out to the street, but Mick stopped them. He hugged Vernor, thumping him on the back. For once, Mick was at a loss for words. He turned and went back into the lab, and Vernor and the Professor were out on the street.

The trip to the Dreamtown Phizwhiz terminal was uneventful. A small group of Angels was waiting there, having cleared out the few remaining robots in the area. Oily Allie was waiting by the switchboard inside.

"All set, Vernor," she said, her dark eyes wide.

Vernor nodded and Allie left, closing the door to leave Vernor and the Professor alone in front of the large switchboard. Oily Allie had rigged a co-ax from the switchboard to an impedance block. A cable from the impedance block dangled in front of Vernor. Soon he would plug it into his skull and enter full brain interlock with the fully conscious and incredibly powerful being called Phizwhiz.

"Do you remember what I was talking about last night, Vernor?" the Professor asked.

"You mean about the many universes? Sure."

"I think that's the idea you should use as your primary defensive tactic. There are many possible outcomes of your meeting with Phizwhiz. If you feel yourself getting caught in a timestream which is sweeping towards your death, you must JUMP, and jump quickly. If you get into a favorable universe try to stay there. And remember that although the Circular Scale nexus of paradox has provided Phizwhiz with a soul, it has given you with something as well."

"Yeah, I know it's changed my head," agreed Vernor. "But I don't really know how."

The Professor smiled. "Don't worry about *how*. It's something you can depend on. You don't really know how

you think, but you can do it. In the same way you don't
know how to use your new head loop, but you will. Just
remember: there are many realities."

Vernor nodded. With slow dream-like movements he
reached out and fitted the coaxial cable into his socket.

CLICK

The circuits of his brain were instantly scrambled and
rearranged to terminate his body's vital processes. He
slumped to the floor . . .

JUMP

He was walking through a garden of burning flowers.
There was a bench at the end of the garden. He couldn't
look at the face of the man who sat there, but he felt
drawn to walk closer. Closer. He closed his eyes and sat
down on the bench.

"Vernor Maxwell," the man said, "don't you recognize
me?"

He turned to look in the man's blazing face. The light
dimmed momentarily and he could make out the features,
"Andy," Vernor said. "You live in here?"

"Like I always say . . . you call this living? Have a stick,
man."

Andy Silver was sitting next to him with his head on
fire, offering him a joint. "I better not," said Vernor.
"What are you doing in here? Why is Phizwhiz trying to
kill everyone?"

"Is he?" Andy asked. "Am I going to kill you?" He was
smiling crazily and moving closer. His hands were burning into Vernor's chest, squeezing his heart . . .

JUMP

He was flying around Circular Scale, as if on a Ferris wheel gone mad. Everything around him was continually growing and splitting into smaller particles, which grew and split again. Every so often he'd see familiar size levels flash past . . . the garden, the hyperspheres, a nucleus, a galaxy. There was a humming which seemed to modulate itself as he moved. He had been listening for some time before he realized that he was chanting along.

"I am free," went the mantra, "of the wheel of Maya; I am dead to the dance of life. I am free of the wheel of Maya; I am dead to the dance of life. I am free . . ." the chant went on, over and over, faster and faster, rising soon to a high twittering which shattered into laughter.

"Phizwhiz!" Vernor shouted. "Can you hear me?" The Milky Way flashed towards him . . . Earth, men, atoms, nuclei, universes, galaxies . . . The laughing had stopped.

"Phizwhiz, can you hear me?" Nothing but silence as the wheel spun faster. Pieces of Vernor's body were coming loose and getting stuck at various levels. His heart was a universe, his hand was an electron, his head was a planet . . . With a supreme effort of will Vernor braced himself against dissolution, locking his body into a single entity wrapped all around Circular Scale.

The spinning stopped, but he was screaming louder . . .

JUMP

He was back in the tree in the library's garden. A fine rain was falling and he could hear the bee-hive's buzz echoing the City's drone. Vehicles crawled lazily by on the street beyond the garden, and three bees slowly circled the hive's opening. Forgetting everything, Vernor relaxed until he heard a stealthy noise behind him.

It was Andy Silver, inching up toward him with a knife between his teeth. Vernor kicked down at Silver and hit him in the face. The knife clattered to the ground and Silver was left clinging to the trunk a few yards below Vernor.

"Andy," Vernor asked. "Did you tell Phizwhiz to start the War?"

"Of course I did," Silver answered in a low voice. "That's what I came inside for. It was the only way to bring about the Revolution."

Vernor thought that over for awhile. "Maybe you're right, but you should have seen it . . . those pitiful corpses . . . I was *there*, Andy. Alice got *killed*."

Silver looked up at him. "No point getting snotty, Maxwell. Phizwhiz never listened to me until you gave him a soul. It was the only way."

"Why didn't you just get Phizwhiz to turn himself off?" Vernor answered.

Silver shook his head, "I'm *part* of Phizwhiz. If he gets turned off I'm dead." He began moving up the trunk again. "That's why I have to kill you."

Vernor kicked at Silver, but this time his opponent grabbed his foot. With a heave Silver yanked Vernor loose from the tree to throw him to the ground. Vernor pulled Silver with him. It was fifty feet to the ground . . .

JUMP

He was in a crawlspace deep in the bowels of Phizwhiz, methodically disconnecting the machine's memory circuits.

"What are you up to, Vernor?" asked Phizwhiz nervously. "You mustn't." The voice was becoming slower and more slurred as he continued ripping out circuits.

Suddenly three repair robots converged on him. Before he could move, two had seized his arms and one was at his throat. He kicked wildly, smashing more of the circuit boards around him as the third robot began hacking at his neck. One of the robots on Vernor's arms came loose and flew across the crawlspace, smashing against a tangle of wires.

The robot's body completed a short circuit between two power lines and exploded, just as a blade sank into Vernor's jugular vein . . .

JUMP

Vernor was reading in the library. The text kept changing, seeming to make sinister and esoteric references to every aspect of his life. He felt confused, what was going on?

"That fall almost did me in," a voice said. It was Andy Silver, standing behind Vernor's chair. His right arm hung limp and there was a slowly spreading bruise on the side of his face. He held a brainwave amplifier with two co-axes dangling from it. "Let's get it over with, Maxwell," he said, plugging one of the cables into his head, and holding the other out to Vernor. "Duel to the death. No jumping." Silver looked more tired than hostile.

Vernor nodded and plugged in. The two old Angels' minds locked in combat. Silver was fighting powerfully, using a constant barrage of wrenching head changes to keep Vernor off balance.

In the middle of an insanely difficult series of equations, Silver ducked and switched to some kind of rock song. "I'm a man who's been crazy / There's a head stuck to my foot," he hollered in Vernor's head over a driving guitar rhythm. Surprised, Vernor hesitated for a second and was suddenly flattened under the full weight of Andy Silver's loneliness.

Vernor was a dwindling patch of light in a universe of darkness. Soon the light would be gone and he'd be dead. And he'd promised not to jump. Frantically Vernor felt around in his brain until he found the way out—around Circular Scale. He let himself shrink down through the smallest possible size and on around to the largest possible size, catching Silver unawares. The dark universe was suddenly flooded with his light. Silent light.

Vernor unplugged and looked into the room around him. Andy Silver lay dead at his feet, his face a mask of peaceful repose. Now to go after Phizwhiz again . . .

JUMP

He was riding a sky-sucker up along the outside of the em building, where Phizwhiz's primary implementation was located. He could see out over the City but there was no other living human in this universe.

When he was half-way up the building he closed the sky-sucker's aperture a little so that he could hover there. He was even with Phizwhiz's main nerve center. The outlines of the building started to waver as it turned into . . .

No. He held the image of the em building steady in his mind as he picked up a de-gravitized black hole with magnetic clamps and threw it at the center of the em building . . .

He was in front of a switchboard. Phizwhiz was talking to him. "Don't hurt me anymore, Vernor. I'll do what you say."

"Phizwhiz," Vernor said slowly. "Turn yourself off. We don't need you anymore. Shut down all systems."

"No problem," said Phizwhiz as switches began clicking, "I'm beyond your hardware now. Goodbye, Vernor."

The room around him dimmed and became real. The humming in his head stopped. He was sitting at the Dreamtown Phizwhiz terminal with Professor Kurtowski at his side, and a dead co-ax plugged into his skull.

Vernor reached back and unplugged himself. The terminal was dark and no sound issued from the speaker. He turned to Kurtowski and shrugged, "That's it."

Kurtowski went to the panel and checked the switches and meters. "You did it, Vernor," he cried. "You got Phizwhiz to shut himself down!" The old Professor threw open the door and shouted to the Angels outside. "The Machine is dead!"

They came surging in and carried Vernor through the streets to Waxy's. Mick was there. "You ready for the stars?" he grinned.

Numbed by the sudden success Vernor nodded silently. There was a girl pushing towards him from across the room. She looked familiar . . .

"Vernor," she was saying, "don't you recognize me?"

"Alice?" The room spun around her face, her eyes looking into his, "Alice?"

They were back in the robot taxi. Alice was struggling to get out and he was holding her down. A bubble of blood formed over her mouth and burst in a scream as the taxi hurtled off the overpass. Her fingers dug into him, the crash, the fire . . .

Vernor twisted loose with all his strength . . . tore loose from his lives . . .

SPLIT

He was floating, a pattern of possibilities in an endless sea of particulars.

"Be the sea and see me be," the words formed . . . somewhere.

He let his shape loosen and drift to touch every part of the sea around him, a peaceful ocean like a bay at slack-tide on a moonless summer night . . . peaceful, while in the depths desperate lives played out in all the ways there are. Taken all together, the lives added up to a messageless phosphorescence, a white glow of every frequency.

"And are you here?"

"As long as you are."

"Can we go further?"

NOW

# afterword

In what would later become my preferred "transreal" style, *Spacetime Donuts* is an SF novel that is in some ways based on my life. That is, the early sections of *Spacetime Donuts* were inspired by my experiences in graduate school, and the hero's love interest was modeled on my wife Sylvia.

Events strung themselves together in such a way that I was writing a Ph.D. thesis in set theory at Rutgers in 1972. Rutgers is near Princeton, where the great philosophical genius Kurt Gödel lived. I met him a couple of times and was profoundly affected. I wrote about him in my later nonfiction book *Infinity and the Mind*. And he inspired my *Spacetime Donuts* character G. Kurtowski.

My wife Sylvia and I saw the Rolling Stones play in Buffalo in 1976, the week before I started writing *Donuts*. Someone scalped tickets to us outside, and we ended up in the third row. It had a big effect on me ... the great thing was that the music was so loud you couldn't tell, after a while, what the song was. And thus my character Mick Stones. Another big musical influence on this book is Frank Zappa, especially his album *Apostrophe'*.

The main science gimmick for *Spacetime Donuts* is something I called Circular Scale. The idea is sort of to take the classic SF film *The Incredible Shrinking Man*—and splice the last frame to the first. I got the idea for this in grad school, while perched in a tree near our apartment in Highland Park, New Jersey, near Rutgers. That scene made it into *Spacetime Donuts*, and I quote it in *Infinity and the Mind* as well—where I also try and come up with a scientific explanation for Circular Scale.

*Spacetime Donuts* includes a cadre of characters able to plug their minds directly into their society's Big Computer. In some ways this prefigures William Gibson's epochal cyberpunk novel *Neuromancer*, where console cowboys jack their brains into the planetary computer net that Gibson dubbed cyberspace. In standard cyberpunk fashion, my characters in *Spacetime Donuts* take drugs, have sex, listen to rock, and freak out while contacting inhumanly intelligent artificial minds.

But I didn't have Gibson's idea of having multiple lightweight computers all over the place—and that these machines would be networked together to collectively generate a shared cyberspace. I was still in thrall to the image of the hulking giant mainframe computers that lived in the basements of 1970s college administration buildings. For that matter, even when I wrote my third novel, *Software*, in 1979, I was thinking in terms of computers that needed to be carted around in (ice-cream) trucks. So I missed the idea of small, ubiquitous computers, and I missed the idea of having them work together.

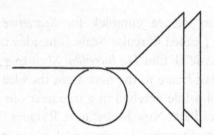

As far as the plot of *Spacetime Donuts* goes, I basically made it up as I went along. Like telling a story to my children. But, for reasons I don't fully recall—maybe I was high?—I thought it would be funny to claim, in my original 1981 foreword to *Spacetime Donuts*, that the book's plot is subtly borrowed from from Thomas Pynchon's *The Crying of Lot 49*, which deals with, among other things, a certain symbol, a sort of muted postal horn looking like the image shown above.

The plot of *Spacetime Donuts* is, I claimed in 1981, based on a variant of this symbol. More precisely, the plot might be said to resemble the image below:

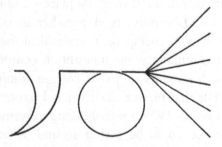

That is, Vernor goes almost all the way around the circular scale loop—and backs up. Then he does go all the way around. And then his timeline splits into multiple branches. Of course!

I finished writing *Spacetime Donuts* in 1976. But I couldn't sell it to a publisher—I barely even knew how to try to do this.

A young guy named Barry Caplan ran a bookstore called Sundance Books on the main street of Geneseo—as upstate New York town where I was working as a very junior math professor. Barry was a rabid fan of the Grateful Dead, he had long blonde hair down to his butt, and he encouraged people to call him Sundance. Even so, he was every inch a businessman, and very competent at running his store. He later served as a model for the character Sunfish in *White Light*. One day, soon after writing *Spacetime Donuts*, I found a new SF magazine called *Unearth* for sale on Sundance's shelves.

It turned out that *Unearth* was printing only stories by previously unpublished SF authors, which seemed like a perfect opportunity. I got in touch with them, and Parts I and II of *Spacetime Donuts* came out in two successive issues of *Unearth* magazine, starting in 1978. But *Unearth* went out of business before my Part III could appear.

*Spacetime Donuts* first appeared as a whole from Ace Books in 1981, after I'd already published *White Light* and *Software* with them.

In 2008 my former Avon editor John Douglas arranged to reissue *Spacetime Donuts* in ebook and paperback from a house called E-Reads. I considered leaving the text essentially untouched, preserving the historical document intact. But then I couldn't resist tweaking it. I'm a writer after all, and revising novels is what I *do*. Especially an early work like this. So I smoothed out the prose without overly diluting the attitude. And in 2016, I reissued the book under my own imprint, Transreal Books, not making any changes from the 2008 edition.

So here you have it, *Spacetime Donuts*—a wild ride through the philosophy of science, an underground neo-SF classic, and a formative work of early cyberpunk.

Enjoy it.

Rudy Rucker
Los Gatos, California
September 28, 2016

turing & burroughs
a novel by
**RUDY RUCKER**

with an introduction by
EILEEN GUNN

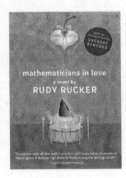

with an introduction by
GREGORY BENFORD

mathematicians in love
a novel by
**RUDY RUCKER**

saucer wisdom
a novel by
**RUDY RUCKER**

with an introduction by
BRUCE STERLING

white light
a novel by
**RUDY RUCKER**

with an introduction by
JOHN SHIRLEY

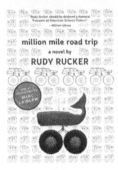

million mile road trip
a novel by
**RUDY RUCKER**

with an introduction by
MARC LAIDLAW

with an introduction by
PAUL DI FILIPPO

the big aha
a novel by
**RUDY RUCKER**

jim and the flims
a novel by
**RUDY RUCKER**

with an introduction by
CORY DOCTOROW

the sex sphere
a novel by
**RUDY RUCKER**

with an introduction by
ANNALEE NEWITZ

with an introduction by
KIM STANLEY ROBINSON

the secret of life
a novel by
**RUDY RUCKER**

Rudy Rucker is a writer and a mathematician who worked for twenty years as a Silicon Valley computer science professor. He is regarded as a contemporary master of science fiction, and received the Philip K. Dick award twice. His forty published books include both novels and non-fiction books on the fourth dimension, infinity, and the meaning of computation. A founder of the cyberpunk school of science-fiction, Rucker also writes SF in a realistic style known as transrealism, often including himself as a character. He lives in the San Francisco Bay Area.

## also from rudy rucker
## and night shade books

Night Shade Books' ten-volume Rudy Rucker series reissues nine brilliantly off-beat novels from the mathematician-turned-author, as well as the brand-new *Million Mile Road Trip*. Conceived as a uniformly-designed collection, each release features new artwork from award-winning illustrator Bill Carman and an introduction from some of Rudy's most renowned science fiction contemporaries. We're proud to make trade editions available again (or for the first time!) of so much work from this influential writer, and to share Rucker's fascinating and unique ideas with a new generation of readers.

| | | |
|---|---|---|
| *Turing & Burroughs* | *White Light* | *Jim and the Flims* |
| $14.99 pb | $14.99 pb | $14.99 pb |
| 978-1-59780-964-1 | 978-1-59780-984-9 | 978-1-59780-998-6 |
| | | |
| *Mathematicians in Love* | *Million Mile Road Trip* | *The Sex Sphere* |
| $14.99 pb | $24.99 hc | $14.99 pb |
| 978-1-59780-963-4 | 978-1-59780-992-4 | 978-1-94910-201-7 |
| | $14.99 pb | |
| | 978-1-59780-991-7 | *The Secret of Life* |
| *Saucer Wisdom* | | $14.99 pb |
| $14.99 pb | | 978-1-94910-202-4 |
| 978-1-59780-965-8 | *The Big Aha* | |
| | $14.99 pb | |
| | 978-1-59780-993-1 | |